PEN PALS:
BOOK FOUR

NO CREEPS
NEED APPLY

by Sharon Dennis Wyeth

A YEARLING BOOK

Published by
Dell Publishing
a division of
Bantam Doubleday Dell Publishing Group, Inc.
666 Fifth Avenue
New York, New York 10103

The trademark Yearling ® is registered in the U.S. Patent and Trademark
Office.

ISBN: 0-440-40241-7
Published by arrangement with Parachute Press, Inc.
Printed in the United States of America
November 1989
10 9 8 7 6 5 4 3 2 1

OPM

For Evon

CHAPTER ONE

"If you could be anywhere in the world right now," Lisa McGreevy asked, "where would you be?"

Twelve-year-old Shanon Davis lifted her intelligent hazel eyes. "I guess I'd be right here working on my Latin," she replied.

"Use your imagination!" Lisa exclaimed. "I'd be anywhere in the world *except* Alma Stephens Boarding School for Girls! I'd be on a desert island or in Paris or climbing a mountain, even on a jungle safari—as long as I was with Rob Williams."

Shanon shook her head and sighed. Ever since the beginning of spring, her thirteen-year-old roommate had been lovesick. And it wasn't as if Rob Williams was even her boyfriend. Rob was Lisa's pen pal from Ardsley Academy. All four of the girls who lived in Fox Hall, Suite 3–D, had pen pals from the nearby boys' school. Advertising for boys to correspond with had been one of the first things the four had done together after starting as freshmen at Alma Stephens.

"Tell the truth," Lisa challenged. "If you could whisk yourself away this minute, wouldn't you want to be with Mars?"

"At Ardsley?" Shanon asked, yawning. She'd been stretched out on her bed studying for a full hour. "Things are even stricter over there than they are here. Mars says they have full-course sit-down dinners three times a week."

"You're missing the point," Lisa insisted. Perching on the windowsill, she scooped up her long dark hair so that the brisk spring breeze could tickle her neck. Though the oversized T-shirt she was wearing was ripped in two places for ventilation, she still felt hot.

"How come your window is open?" an imperious voice demanded. "It's downright freezing in here!"

Palmer Durand, Lisa and Shanon's blonde suitemate, stalked into the bedroom, her arms full of clothing. "There!" she announced, dumping the load on Lisa's bed. "I've done it!"

"What's the idea?" Lisa exclaimed. "Isn't it enough that you hog all the closet space from Amy in your own room?"

"I don't want to use your closet space," Palmer said brightly. "These are give-aways!"

"Wow!" Shanon gulped. The only new thing she'd been able to afford for spring was a pair of sneakers. Some of the clothes in Palmer's pile still had the price tags on them!

"I still want to know what the big idea is," Lisa said suspiciously. If there was one trait Palmer Durand *wasn't* known for in Suite 3–D it was her generosity. Lisa

2

wondered how Amy Ho, Palmer's roommate, could put up with her. Lisa and Shanon only had to share the sitting room with the self-absorbed junior debutante, but Amy had to sleep in the same bedroom with her.

"I'm in a good mood today," Palmer said. "I just got a letter from Simmie! When Amy gets back, I'll read it to all of you. It's *so* excellent!"

"Mars hasn't written to me in two whole weeks," Shanon murmured, going through the big stack of clothes. "May I try on this lavender polo?" she asked shyly.

"Take anything you like," Palmer encouraged. "You, too, Lisa. There's a pair of toreadors you might be interested in."

"Since when do you wear toreadors?" Lisa said, eyeing the clothes from a distance. Usually Palmer's taste was ultra-conservative.

"I bought them as an experiment," she replied, grabbing the pants from the pile. "But they're too loud for me." She held them out to Lisa—they were red with black stripes. "They'd look great on you, though!"

"Why do you want to give them to me?" Lisa asked.

"Because I like you." Palmer gave her a wounded look. "Anyone would think you didn't trust me."

"Thanks anyway," Lisa said, "but red's not my color." Actually, red was Lisa's favorite color, and the pants would've looked terrific on her. But she didn't want to take Palmer's cast-offs. Lately, Palmer had done a number of underhanded things to hurt Lisa's feelings, and it wasn't that easy to forget them. Besides, it irked Lisa that Palmer's mother gave her an unlimited charge account. Though

3

Lisa's family was probably just as wealthy, they still sent her a set—and modest—monthly allowance.

"Here comes Amy!" Shanon announced, looking out of the window. Down below, Amy Ho streaked across the quadrangle and into Fox Hall. Though Lisa was probably the most naturally athletic of the girls in the suite, Amy was the one who invested the most in physical fitness. Besides playing soccer and softball, she jogged daily and did calisthenics. She also composed rock music and played the guitar. Shanon's extracurricular interest was writing stories for Alma's newspaper, *The Ledger*, while Lisa involved herself in various art projects. Palmer was the only one in the suite without a hobby.

"Hey, Foxes!" Amy called, slamming the outside door to the suite. "Where are you?" Foxes of the Third Dimension was the code name the girls had used in their ad for pen pals, and in private they still called themselves the Foxes. The four Ardsley boys they wrote to called themselves The Unknown.

"We're in here!" Lisa yelled from the room she shared with Shanon.

Amy appeared in the doorway. Her lovely oval face was flushed from exercise, her almond-shaped eyes were shining, and her usually spiked black hair was smoothed back.

"You must have taken the stairs by threes to get up here so fast," Lisa said. "Did you stop at Booth Hall to check my mailbox for me?"

"Sure did!" Amy replied, still breathless.

"I love your jogging clothes," Shanon said, admiring the fantastic black spandex suit with gold dragons on it.

4

"Thanks," Amy said. "My aunt in Taiwan sent it for my thirteenth birthday. Got a towel?" she asked, taking a seat among the clothes on the bed.

"Watch out!" Palmer shouted. "You're crushing the merchandise!"

Amy grinned and moved over an inch. "What is this? A rummage sale?"

"Palmer's emptying out her closet," Lisa quipped, tossing a towel over.

"Fabulous," Amy said wryly. "Now maybe there'll be some room for *my* things."

"Actually, I've ordered a few new outfits to take the place of these," Palmer said hurriedly. "My spring wardrobe has got to be just right for Simmie. Wait till you hear what he wrote me." She pulled a piece of paper out of her skirt pocket. "It's the most wonderful—"

"Let Amy catch her breath," Lisa commanded. "Anyway, she may have a letter for me. Do you?" she asked eagerly.

"You're in luck," Amy answered, taking an envelope out of her waist pouch.

Lisa snatched the letter from Amy's hand. "It's from Rob! I knew he'd write!"

"Anything in my mailbox?" Shanon asked.

"Sorry," Amy replied. "Nothing from Mars."

"It's been ages since he's written," Shanon said with a worried expression.

"It's been a while since John's written, too," Amy said thoughtfully.

"Well, *I* got a letter from Simmie!" Palmer exclaimed.

5

"That is, if anybody's interested. . . ." And standing in the center of the room, she started to read:

Dear Palmer—

"Wait!" Lisa gasped. She stood up breathlessly. "You have to hear this first! Just listen to what Rob wrote! It's what I've been waiting for!"

"Simmie's letter is what I've been waiting for, too!" Palmer said angrily.

The two girls glared at each other. Palmer's blue eyes were ice and Lisa's dark ones were fire.

"Maybe we should find a way of taking turns," Shanon suggested diplomatically.

"Palmer did start first," Amy pointed out.

"Go ahead," Lisa muttered.

Palmer hesitated a moment. "No, you go first," she said, forcing a magnanimous smile. "I don't mind waiting."

"Thanks," Lisa said, surprised. It wasn't like Palmer to take a back seat. Maybe she *was* feeling generous. "This won't take a minute," she added excitedly.

Dear Lisa,
I was glad to get your last letter. I have had some interesting news from my father. I told you once that every summer he gets me a job with one of his friends in some interesting place. This year he has given me two choices. I can either go to work on a dairy farm in Pennsylvania or go back to Alaska and work for Dad's friend who raises musk ox. In any case I'll be mooing or snorting all the

6

time. The thing is that the musk ox experience was excellent, but I've already done it. However, a dairy farm in Pennsylvania might not be as exciting. Anyway, that's all my news for now. Catch you later.

Rob

"Isn't that amazing!" Lisa exclaimed.

"How so?" Amy asked.

"Rob has a chance to work in Pennsylvania this summer," she said excitedly. "I *live* in Pennsylvania. This summer I'll be at home and Rob will be working in the same state. I'll get to see him!"

"On a dairy farm?" Shanon said doubtfully.

"Who cares?" Lisa said happily. "We'd be living in the same state."

"It's a pretty big state," Amy pointed out.

"I could get my father to drive me over to visit him," Lisa insisted. "This is the chance I've been waiting for. Too bad nobody else thinks it's as exciting as I do," she added, pouting.

"I think it's very exciting!" Palmer said encouragingly. "Now all you have to do is convince *Rob* that Pennsylvania is more exciting than Alaska. You could look up Pennsylvania in the encyclopedia. I'm sure there are lots of great things about your state that you don't even know. I'd be glad to help you do some research on it."

"What a terrific idea!" Lisa agreed. "You'd help me?"

"Sure," Palmer said, smiling broadly. "I think your scheme to spend more time with Rob is smart. Wait until you hear my plan about Simmie!"

7

"What plan?" Amy asked.

Palmer blushed and smiled. "Let me read his letter. Then maybe you'll know what I'm talking about." A lock of blonde hair fell across one blue eye as she bent over the crumpled note from Simmie Randolph III. As she read his words, her voice took on a tone of reverence.

Hey, Gorgeeous,
You will finally get a chance to see me play tennis. Hate to brag, but I am a great player. Anyway, the coach is sending me to the round robin exhibition thing you girls are having at Alma. You will probably be in it, too, since you are such a good tennis player. It's going to be mixed doubles. See you on the court.

Simmie

Palmer tossed her head triumphantly. "So what do you think?"

"Let me see that," Amy said, taking the note. "In the first line he misspelled the word 'gorgeous.' "

"I certainly know what he means by it," Palmer snapped at her. "What's more important is that this is the perfect way of getting to know Simmie better. The perfect way of spending time with him!"

Shanon twisted a strand of her light brown hair. "You're going to enter the round robin?" she ventured.

"That's the plan," Palmer replied.

"That's ridiculous!" Amy said bluntly. "You don't even play tennis."

"But I do!" Palmer exclaimed. "My mother was one of

the best players here in the old days when she went to Alma!"

"What does your mother have to do with it?" Lisa asked.

"My mother likes tennis more than anything else in the world," Palmer told them. "Every single summer of my life I've had to go to tennis camp. We even have our own tennis court at home."

"But you've never even mentioned tennis before," Amy argued.

Palmer shrugged. "That's because I never liked it. Anyway, I did mention tennis to Simmie. When I found out that tennis was one of his favorite sports, I told him it was mine too."

"Oh, brother," said Lisa. "Something tells me this isn't going to work. How can you make yourself like something just because a boy likes it?"

"You want Rob to like Pennsylvania just because you live there," Shanon pointed out.

"I don't see where the situations are similar," Lisa objected.

"Who cares whether they are or not?" Amy put in. "I think it's great that Palmer has an interest in something, whatever the reason."

"That's right," Palmer said. "Everybody's always encouraging me to develop an interest. So now I'm interested in tennis. And I've ordered eleven new tennis outfits."

"Eleven!" Shanon gasped, while Amy and Lisa exchanged glances.

"I can't help it if we're stuck up in the hills of New

Hampshire, miles from a store," Palmer countered. "I have to buy more than I need when I order from a catalogue. Otherwise, how can I be sure anything will fit?"

Amy rolled her eyes and laughed. After several months of living in the same room, she was getting used to Palmer's strange logic. In fact, she'd actually begun to like her, even though the two of them were as different as oil and water. "It's going to take work to get on the tennis team," Amy cautioned. "Coach Barker is no pushover."

"I know I can do it!" Palmer insisted. "Especially if I have help. . . ." She turned her gaze to Lisa.

"Uh-oh," Lisa said. "Whose help did you have in mind?"

"Yours, of course," Palmer said sweetly. "You are a fantastic tennis player, aren't you?"

Lisa shrugged. "Like you, I've played all my life."

"So before I go out for the team, you can coach me!" Palmer said as if that were the most natural thing in the world.

"Me, coach you?" Lisa couldn't believe her ears. "Sorry!—I haven't got time!"

"Why not?" Amy asked, jumping in. "You could at least go to the court with Palmer a few mornings and help her brush up. This is the first time Palmer has ever gone out for something."

"And she offered to help you research Pennsylvania for Rob," Shanon reminded her.

Lisa took a few steps backward. All three of the other Foxes were staring at her.

"Pretty please," Palmer begged.

10

"Oh, okay!" Lisa gave in grudgingly. "We'll give it a try first thing tomorrow." Crossing to the bed, she snatched up the red and black toreadors. If she was going to spend her mornings with Palmer Durand, the least she was going to get out of it was a pair of pants!

Dear Rob,

Your job possibilities for the summer sound incredible, especially the one in Pennsylvania! I can think of nothing more exciting than working on a dairy farm! And Pennsylvania is beautiful in the summer! If you have any questions about it, don't hesitate to ask. Remember, that's where I come from! And I'll be there this summer!

Yours truly,
Lisa

Dear Simmie,

Good news! I am in training for the round robin mixed doubles. See you in a few weeks on the tennis court!

Yours truly,
Palmer

P.S. Gorgeous is spelled with one "e."

11

CHAPTER TWO

———————◆———————

Amy played "Strawberry Fields" on her guitar while Shanon hummed along.

"Cut it out for a minute," Lisa muttered. Amy stopped and put down her guitar. The three girls had been waiting under the trees by the tennis courts for half an hour.

"If Palmer's not here in five more minutes," Lisa warned, "I'm leaving! Every single time we've practiced, she's been late."

"I'm sure there's an explanation," Shanon volunteered, trying to smooth things over.

"Sure," Lisa said, "like she couldn't decide what to wear. She comes to these practice sessions as if she's already at Wimbledon."

"She's very excited about it," Amy said loyally.

"Well, I'm excited about my photography project," countered Lisa, "and instead of being in the darkroom, I'm out here—waiting for Palmer! Not only that, I haven't even started my history paper for Mr. Seganish."

As Amy picked up her guitar and began to strum again,

Palmer waltzed over in sparkling tennis whites. "Hi, everyone!" she called cheerfully.

"You're late!" Lisa greeted her.

"Sorry," Palmer said carelessly. "At the last minute I thought my hair needed washing."

"That's the reason you kept me waiting?" Lisa sputtered.

"Why don't you just get on with the practice?" Shanon suggested.

"Is that a new racket?" Amy asked, stepping in.

"It arrived yesterday," Palmer replied, taking a swing.

"Great," Amy said. "I hope it helps you."

"Can we quit the small talk and start?" Lisa grumbled. "A new racket's not going to do you any good without a backhand."

"I thought you said my backhand was improving," Palmer snapped.

"Let's see how it is this morning," Lisa said grandly.

"Okay!" Palmer countered. "Why don't I show you?"

Amy and Shanon watched them stalk onto a court together. "Maybe this wasn't the greatest idea," Shanon admitted.

Amy giggled. "You're right. Lisa looks like she'd rather hit Palmer than a tennis ball."

Palmer and Lisa warmed up with a rally, tossed for the serve, then began to play seriously. "Palmer's definitely improving," Amy observed.

"She's quick, all right," Shanon agreed. "She looks almost as good as Lisa."

"I never thought she'd be that coordinated," said Amy. "It's remarkable," she added as a tall, athletic-looking

13

woman approached the court. She was in her twenties, with curly red hair and big blue eyes.

"Isn't that Coach Barker?" Shanon asked Amy. "She was here the other day watching, wasn't she?"

"Yes," Amy said. "Maybe she's interested in Palmer. I've heard she's looking for fresh blood on the tennis team."

"Hey there, Ho," Coach Kathy Barker greeted Amy.

"Hey, Coach," Amy replied.

Shanon looked away shyly. All the coaches knew Amy; none of them knew who Shanon was.

"Hey, Davis," Coach Barker said, surprising her.

Shanon smiled as the coach stood next to them for a few minutes.

"She's good," Coach Barker said, staring intently at the court where Lisa and Palmer were practicing.

"She wants to go out for the tennis team!" Shanon volunteered brightly.

The coach smiled thoughtfully. "Is that so? I could use somebody like that. When she's ready, tell her to talk to me."

"Did you hear that?" Shanon said once the coach had walked away. "Palmer's got it made! The coach is interested in her!"

"Are you sure she wasn't talking about Lisa?" Amy asked doubtfully. "She was watching both of them."

"No," said Shanon. "She was definitely watching Palmer. I saw her. Anyway, she knows Lisa's already gone out for crew."

Lisa and Palmer walked off the court smiling. Playing the game had changed their moods.

14

"You're getting hard to beat," Lisa said.

Palmer flushed. "Thanks for helping me."

"Guess what?" Amy volunteered. "Coach Barker was watching Palmer and thought she was pretty good."

"Wow!" Palmer said.

"She said when you were ready to go out for the team, you should talk to her," Shanon added.

"I can't believe it!" Palmer squeaked. "And it's all thanks to you, Lisa."

Shanon beamed. It made her feel good when everybody was getting along together.

"It's your hard work," Lisa said modestly. "You did—" She broke off suddenly as Kate Majors joined the group.

"Fancy meeting you here," the older girl said. "Why aren't you in class?"

"Our classes aren't until later," Shanon explained dutifully.

Lisa eyed Kate's dweeby outfit. She was dressed in a wool skirt even though it was spring. "Aren't you hot?" Lisa asked.

"Not really," Kate said, pushing her glasses up. In one arm she was holding a full bookbag, and Lisa found this irritating. It was bad enough that Kate studied so much— she didn't have to show it off by carrying a ton of books around all the time. But the most irritating thing about Kate was the fact that she'd recently become friendly with Lisa's brother Reggie, who went to Ardsley.

"So how's my brother these days?" Lisa asked. "Not that he ever writes or calls me."

"He's fine," Kate replied, blushing. Her face got even redder as her green bookbag suddenly began moving.

15

"What's in your bag?" Palmer asked, backing away. "Do you have something alive in there?"

Kate gulped nervously and looked around. "I guess it's all right if I show you," she said, coming closer. "But you mustn't tell anybody."

"What is it?" Amy asked curiously.

Kate loosened the top of her bag, and the four girls moved closer. The soft head of a calico kitten emerged from the top. "Her name is Tickle," Kate whispered. "I found her a couple of days ago, wandering on the street next to the quadrangle."

"She's beautiful," Shanon said with a sigh. "My cat at home is calico."

"I thought pets were against the rules," Lisa said devilishly.

"I thought so, too," Palmer agreed.

As the monitor on their floor in Fox Hall, Kate Majors had proven to be a real stickler about the rules. Palmer and Lisa were delighted to see her breaking one for a change.

"Pets may be against the rules," Kate admitted, "but this rule is unfair to animals. I'm only keeping Tickle until she finds a good home. And if you breathe a word of it to anybody"—she gave them a threatening glare—"I'll tell some things *I* know about."

"We won't tell," Shanon volunteered. Though Kate had been hard on the Foxes in the beginning of the school year, she hadn't given them any trouble since then.

"No, far be it from us to be tattletales," Lisa said, waltzing away.

"Going for a shower?" Palmer called. "I'll join you."

16

As they headed back toward the dorm, Lisa and Palmer didn't say much. On the court they'd had fun together, but now that they were just walking, they both felt uncomfortable. There had been too much bad feeling between the two girls for it to disappear instantly.

"Do you really think I've improved?" Palmer asked, forcing a smile.

"Yes, I do," Lisa replied. "Are you going to talk to Coach Barker?"

"The next time I get a chance," Palmer said. "I'm so glad you think I'm good. Simmie's a great player, and I have to be good enough for him."

"I hope you're not just brushing up on your game for him," Lisa lectured. "Showing off on the court is not going to win you any points."

"Thanks for the advice," Palmer snapped, "but I don't think I need it."

"Great," Lisa said. "Does that go for the coaching, too?"

"Sure," Palmer said haughtily. "I can handle myself now that Coach Barker has noticed me."

"If you don't mind, I'm in a hurry," Lisa muttered, breaking into a run. It was just like Palmer Durand to be so unappreciative!

"See you later," Palmer called after her. Watching Lisa take off, she wanted to follow. But she was too proud. Lisa McGreevy took every opportunity to humiliate her. It was a miracle that she had agreed to help at all. And as for Lisa's know-it-all advice about not playing for Simmie's benefit, Palmer thought that was absolute rubbish. What better inspiration did she need to win the round robin exhibition than a tall, blonde, handsome fourteen-year-old guy from Ardsley Academy? What could possibly be more inspiring than Simmie Randolph III?

"Have you noticed how moody Lisa's been these days?" Shanon asked Amy on their way to Booth Hall. The two girls were going to check their mail and get the thick chocolatey shakes they called choc-shots. Then Shanon would be off to French with Miss Grayson and Amy to her advanced math class.

"Palmer's moody, too," Amy said. "And come to think of it, I haven't been myself lately either."

"Neither have I," Shanon confessed.

Amy shrugged. "Maybe it's spring fever."

Arriving at Booth, they pushed through the double doors. The front corridor had a big bulletin board covered with notices. To the left were the student mailboxes, and down the hall was the snack bar.

"My heart pounds a lot," Shanon said, opening her mailbox. "And sometimes I feel tingly all over."

"I feel that way, too," Amy said. "Like I can't breathe deep enough and I want to keep jumping." She pulled an envelope out of her box. "Hurray, I got something today!"

"Nothing for me," Shanon said glumly. She wondered what was going on with Mars. Why hadn't he written her? It wasn't as if she had a gigantic crush on him the way Lisa had on Rob, but she did like him—a lot.

The girls ambled into the snack bar and ordered their choc-shots. Beyond the open windows, they could see the

18

budding forsythia. Shanon took off her jacket and Amy unbuttoned her sweater. In line with the Alma dress code for classes, they were both wearing skirts and blouses.

"I shouldn't be drinking this," Shanon sighed, sinking her straw into the shake. "But whether my face breaks out or not, today I crave chocolate."

"Me, too," Amy said. "Must be another symptom of spring fever. I got a letter from John. Listen—"

Dear Amy,
   I have thought of you often and am sorry that I've been too busy to write. But this current poem I am working on has been torture. I couldn't get it right. But now, if I say so myself, it's perfect. Take a gander and tell me what you think. I want you to be perfectly honest.
   Declaration of Independence, by John Adams
   The drifting moon follows me
   It is woman
   Reason, can't I get along without you?
   Giant worm boring into my soul!
   In this age man does all
   Frolics, builds planes, plays ball, climbs mountains
   All these alone, save write a song.
   Would I were in no need of her here also!
   Cruel muse, I'd do better alone.

"What do you think?" Shanon asked, with a puzzled frown.

"I hate it! John's writing is usually better." Amy slurped her shake.

"Are you going to tell him that?" Shanon asked.

"Why not? He told me to be perfectly honest."

The fragrance of early spring wafted gently through the windows. The calm before the storm.

Dear John,

I do not like your poem. Not only do I find it hard to follow, but I think it is insulting to women. Hope you are well otherwise. The flowers are blooming up here. Is it warmer down in the valley? I am finding the Beatles are quintessential. I haven't written any songs lately. Have you?

Yours truly,
Amy

Dear Mars,

How are you? I hope you are okay. Why haven't you written to me? I am getting worried. Don't you want to be pen pals anymore? Write soon.

Sincerely,
Shanon

CHAPTER THREE

———◆———

A fierce wind stung Palmer's bare legs as she slammed her ball against the backboard of the practice court. March had come in like a lamb but only for a few brief balmy days. Being from Florida, Palmer hated the chilly weather, but she was determined to make the tennis team. She had put off talking to Coach Barker until she was sure she was perfect. And now as she chased the ball back and forth, her blue eyes glazed over in dreamy anticipation. . . .

On the morning of the round robin exhibition, Simmie Randolph III would step off the bus from Ardsley Academy. He would be wearing white tennis shorts and a white polo. His thick golden hair would fall over one eye just as it did in the poster-sized photo hanging over Palmer's bed. When he came over to say hello, he would smile at her and his sea-green eyes would glint in the sun. Coach Barker would pair her with him for the exhibition, and together they would win! While they walked hand in hand off the court, he would ask her to the Ardsley dance! She would wear her new blue dress with the glittery things on it. She would look better than anybody, and he would ask her to be his girlfriend! If, that is, she made the tennis team.

If she didn't make the team, Palmer knew, it would all be different. Simmie would still be there in his whites, but he would be shocked to find that Palmer was not even playing. She would have to explain how she'd lied about being a great tennis player, how she'd had to work at it with the help of Lisa; how she wasn't in the round robin after all. Simmie wouldn't smile. He would snarl. He would walk away, and she would be totally humiliated—

The ball spun out into the air and flew past Palmer's racket. Her dreamy blue eyes had lost focus. The words of Simmie's last letter drummed through her brain . . .

Hey Palmer babe,

The news that you are going to be in the round robin is terrific. You and I will make a great team. The captain of our squad is a buddy of mine who will do anything for me, so I think I can fix it so that we are paired. It'll be an eternity until I see you again. I will be playing with the most gorgeous (I spelled it right this time) girl at Alma.

Yours sincerely,
Simmie

"So what's the weather prediction?" a voice rang out behind her.

Palmer whirled around. She was face to face with Coach Barker. "What . . . what did you say?"

Barker smiled wryly. "You were staring up at the clouds.

22

What do you think? Are we going to get snow?"

"I hope not," Palmer gulped. She couldn't believe she'd missed her chance to impress the coach! Like an idiot, she'd just been standing there in the middle of the court.

"So what are you doing with that racket?" Coach Barker asked. "Planning to go a few rounds with this wind we've got?"

"I've been playing . . . by myself," Palmer blurted.

"So what do you think of yourself?" Barker said with a half smile. "Are you a worthy opponent?"

Palmer looked at her dumbly. Something about the coach's sharp blue eyes made her nervous. Nobody else at Alma had ever done that, not her teachers, not even the headmistress Miss Pryn.

"It's a joke," the coach explained. "I always find solo practice sessions tough. It takes willpower."

Palmer shivered. While she was practicing, she'd felt hot in her sweater. Now it wasn't enough to keep her warm. "I've been doing a lot of hitting," she said, working up her courage. Now was the perfect time to tell Coach Barker she was going out for the team. "You sent a message to me the other day . . ." she began.

"Did I?" said the coach, tugging at her Windbreaker. "I said I wanted to speak with McGreevy."

"Lisa McGreevy?" Palmer asked, startled.

Coach Barker nodded. "She wants to go out for the tennis team. I've been watching her."

Palmer's face got hot. "Yes, she's been out here a lot, practicing with me."

"McGreevy's got tremendous potential," the coach continued. "But I know she's already on crew. I was surprised to hear she had time for tennis as well."

"I'm surprised, too," Palmer muttered.

"Anyway, tell McGreevy to come and see me," the coach said again. "By the way, Durand, you're a good player, too."

"My mother used to play for the Alma tennis team," Palmer managed to say.

The coach smiled. "I know about that. Not your game, though?"

"I guess not," she said. "Not with people like Lisa competing."

"See you around," Barker said. "I'm freezing. Don't catch the flu out here."

Once the coach was out of sight, Palmer threw down her racket. Inside she was boiling with anger. So now Lisa had decided to go out for the team, too! Of all the dirty, rotten tricks!

Lisa's hands were shaking. She was holding Rob's latest letter. "What do you think I should do?" she asked Amy and Shanon.

"Take a walk and clear your mind," Amy suggested.

"Work on your history paper," Shanon advised.

"How can I do either of those things?" Lisa wailed. She threw herself down on the pink loveseat that Shanon's folks had donated for the girls' sitting room.

"You're making too much of it," Amy said, picking up her guitar.

"Please don't start strumming now," Lisa commanded. "Not while I'm having a breakdown."

24

"How about a cup of tea?" Shanon offered. "I could boil some water with the heating coil."

"No," Lisa said tearfully. She looked at Rob's letter again. "I guess this is the end of everything."

"How can you say that?" Amy argued.

"Read it!" Lisa said. "It's right there in his own handwriting!"

Amy sighed and took the letter. "I'll read it again," she said patiently.

Dear Lisa,

Thanks for your suggestion, but I have decided to go back to Alaska this summer. Compared to working with musk ox, working on a dairy farm will be boring. Write soon. I guess you've heard about the dance coming up at Ardsley.

Yours truly,
Rob

"You see!" Lisa moaned. "It's horrible."

"Why is it horrible?" Amy said, losing her patience. "He says he wants you to write to him."

"He even mentions the dance," Shanon volunteered.

"Neither of you understands!" Lisa exclaimed. "Rob had the perfect opportunity to be working where I'm going to be this summer and he didn't take it! It proves that he doesn't like me!"

"How can you say that?" Shanon protested. "Rob gave you his freshman pin at the Strawberry Breakfast!"

"So what?" Lisa wailed. "What's a class pin mean these days anyway? Ardsley is probably the only boys' school

25

left in the entire country that still gives out class pins! Rob probably just wanted to get rid of his!"

"Aren't you being a little over-dramatic?" Shanon said.

"She certainly is," Amy asserted. "Rob Williams has always written very friendly letters to you. And he never, ever wrote that he didn't like you."

"He did!" Lisa shouted in frustration. "A letter is not only in the words a person writes! You have to read what's between the lines! And it's clear to me—"

Before Lisa could finish her thought, there was a sharp knock at the door.

"What's all the yelling about?" Kate asked, sticking her head into the suite.

"We're having a discussion," Shanon said nervously.

Kate slipped inside and shut the door behind her. Lisa noticed a squirming bump under Kate's sweater.

"What are you hiding? Did you bring that kitten in here?" Lisa demanded.

"I need a favor," Kate said, avoiding Lisa and walking over to Shanon. "Keep Tickle for an hour or so. Dolores is coming to my room, and I don't trust her."

"But Dolores is your friend," Shanon said, puzzled.

"She's also a stickler about rules," Kate confided.

"Even more than you are?" Amy asked.

"Even more than I am," Kate replied earnestly. Her gray eyes had a pleading look. "I've overlooked a lot for this suite. Can't you do me a favor for once?"

"Of course we can," Shanon said, getting up to take the kitten. "Tickle can stay here as long as she likes."

Lisa turned away. She didn't want Kate, of all people, to

see how upset she was. Kate might tell Reggie about it, and Lisa didn't want her brother hearing any secondhand news about her.

"Thanks a lot," Kate said gratefully. "And whatever you were discussing before, you'd better keep it down, or Miss Grayson will be up here. You know how she is about bickering. Why don't you concentrate on your homework or something? I happen to know that a couple of you have been scoring low on your quizzes. And don't forget to wear skirts tonight. There's a sit-down dinner—"

"Thanks for your advice," Lisa shot over her shoulder, "but I thought you had a meeting with Dolores in your room."

"I get the hint," Kate mumbled, heading for the door. "What a grouch. If it wasn't for your brother—"

Palmer barged in as Kate slipped out.

"There you are!" Palmer exclaimed, glaring at Lisa. "What a rat! What a traitor!"

"Maybe we'd better get a pair of boxing gloves," Amy quipped. "Chill out, Palmer. Kate just warned us to keep it down."

"How dare you call me a traitor," Lisa challenged loudly, ignoring Amy's advice. "After all I've done to help you!"

"You weren't helping me at all!" Palmer said bitterly. "You were helping yourself. Coach Barker told me all about your going out for the tennis team!"

Lisa's mouth dropped open. "How could Coach Barker say that when it's not true?"

"It *is* true," Palmer said. "And all the time I thought you

27

were trying to be my friend. But you were just playing a trick on me! You probably want to play in the round robin with Simmie yourself."

"I could care less about Simmie Randolph," Lisa sputtered. "It's Rob that I care about! But in case you're interested, I've just found out that he doesn't care about me! So I have enough to worry about without you giving me a hard time."

Amy got up and raised both arms. "Hold it!" she bellowed.

Everyone froze. Lisa and Palmer were squared off in the middle of the room, while Shanon sat scrunched up on the loveseat.

"I think we have to talk about some stuff," Amy said seriously. "I don't know about Shanon, but I'm sick and tired of hearing about Rob Williams and Simmie Randolph."

"That's because you're not as serious about John," Palmer said huffily.

"I like John," Amy insisted. "I enjoy writing to him. But he's not the only thing in the world I think about."

"That's because your relationship is perfect," Lisa argued. "All you do is write friendly letters."

"No they don't," Shanon piped up. "Amy wrote a letter to John just recently saying that she didn't like a poem he wrote."

"You did?" Lisa asked in amazement. "That was brave. John is very sensitive about his poetry. Did he answer you back yet?"

"Not yet," Amy said. "But I'm sure that whatever he

28

says, I'm not going to be upset about it."

"That just proves that what Lisa said is right," Palmer spoke up. "Your relationship with John is completely different. I'd do anything in the world for Simmie! Anything!"

"Would you jump in a river?" Amy challenged.

Palmer rolled her eyes. "Anything within reason is what I meant. Just look how I'm working to get on the tennis team. And I thought I stood a good chance until I found out Lisa was stabbing me in the back."

"I'm not stabbing you in the back!" Lisa said angrily. "You must be crazy!"

"Palmer's not crazy," Shanon groaned, "but *I* will be if all this fighting doesn't stop."

"Fine," Lisa said. "I'll go to my room and get changed for dinner. I'm sorry that you and Amy don't understand why Rob is so important to me. I guess you've just never been in love," she finished, before stalking into the bedroom and slamming the door.

"In love?" Amy sniffed. "She hardly knows him."

"What does that have to do with it?" Palmer said. "For once Lisa has expressed my sentiments exactly. If she's in love with Rob, then I'm in love with Simmie! Too bad you and Shanon don't feel the same way about John and Mars. You'd be much happier."

Then Palmer walked into her bedroom and shut the door firmly.

"The whole suite is breaking up," Shanon wailed.

"Good thing they don't actually go to school with Rob and Simmie," Amy said. "Then they'd really go crazy."

Shanon grabbed her jacket off a hook. "I'm glad I'm already dressed for dinner. I just can't face Lisa when she's like this."

"Don't you have waitress duty at dinner tonight?" Amy asked.

Shanon nodded.

"You'd better go," Amy directed. "Mrs. Butter doesn't like her helpers to be late."

"See you over there," Shanon said, heading out the door. She stopped when she noticed Tickle. "Kate's cat is still here."

"Don't worry. I'll sneak her back when the coast is clear," Amy said. "And try not to take it so hard about Lisa and Palmer," she added.

"I'll try," Shanon said, biting her nails, "but I like things when they're peaceful."

"Me, too," Amy agreed. "I can see getting excited like this about some things—but not boys!"

CHAPTER FOUR

The dining-hall tables were set with spanking white cloths and there was a name card at each place. Dressed in skirts and fresh blouses, Amy, Palmer, and Lisa filed in. Every other Sunday, supper was sit-down, complete with student-waitress service.

"I hope we get Shanon for our waitress," Lisa said, checking out the name cards. "Look, we're all seated at the same table."

"Great," Palmer drawled sarcastically. "I can't think of any better company." Her eyes narrowed in Lisa's direction.

Lisa returned the glare, then sat down at the table and folded her arms tightly across her chest.

"Here comes Mr. Griffith," Amy exclaimed, trying to be cheerful. "He's going to be at our table."

The girls' handsome English teacher strolled over and took the seat next to Lisa. "Good evening, ladies." His deep voice floated across the table.

Lisa muttered a flat hello, and Palmer whispered a hi. Amy rolled her eyes at her suitemates. She knew things must be pretty bad if even Mr. Griffith couldn't get a rise out of them.

"Is Miss Grayson going to be at our table?" Amy asked brightly. Lisa, Palmer, Amy, and Shanon firmly believed that Miss Grayson and Mr. Griffith were in love with each other. Detecting signs of the attraction between the two teachers was one of their favorite pastimes.

"Miss Grayson won't be at our table tonight," Mr. Griffith replied, clearing his throat. He cast his eyes toward the other end of the dining hall where the young French teacher was already seated at a table with Mr. Seganish, one of the history teachers. "Coach Barker will be with us."

Palmer stiffened. "I can't stay!" she whispered to Amy.

"What are you talking about?" Amy whispered back. "Don't be dumb. This is your chance to—"

Just then, Coach Barker took a seat, followed by Kate Majors and another older girl, Brenda Smith. This was Brenda's second year on the tennis team.

"Thanks for taking care of my you-know-what," Kate spoke softly into Lisa's ear as she took the empty seat beside her.

"Don't thank me," Lisa replied crossly.

Amy surveyed the group around the table. Nobody was saying anything but a lot was going on: Lisa and Palmer were still definitely mad at each other, Lisa's arms were still tensely folded, and Palmer's hand was now clenching her fork. Kate looked uncomfortably guilty about

32

something—probably Tickle—and Brenda looked just plain uncomfortable. And no wonder, Amy thought, considering the dirty looks Palmer was throwing her way. Palmer must be jealous of everyone on the tennis team. Even Mr. Griffith seemed restless. His green eyes kept wandering toward the other end of the hall where Miss Grayson was sitting. Coach Barker was the only one who seemed happy with the seating arrangements.

"Nice to see you, McGreevy," the coach said, beaming at Lisa.

Palmer shifted uncomfortably.

"Fancy meeting you twice in the same day, Durand," Barker added.

"Aren't we a happy group?" Mr. Griffith interrupted, turning his gaze back to the table. "I wonder where our food is. Everyone else seems to be eating."

"Here it comes!" Kate volunteered, spotting Shanon.

Shanon sailed toward their table with a tray full of salads.

"Sorry I kept you waiting," she mumbled nervously. Her wait-on wasn't going well. She'd already dropped one dish in the kitchen.

"That's okay," Amy assured her. "I don't think Palmer and Lisa feel like eating anyway."

As Shanon observed the tense group, her brow furrowed with worry. Palmer and Lisa were still having their fight, she thought, before rushing back to the kitchen.

"You seem fidgety today, love," Mrs. Worth, the cook, sang out from the range. "Calm down a bit."

"I've got faculty at my table," Shanon explained, arranging her entrees frantically. The other waitresses had already come and gone with their trays. But Shanon couldn't seem to fit all her plates on. Maybe it was because the main dish was Rock Cornish game hens.

Mrs. Worth lifted an eyebrow. "Let me help, dearie." Plopping a neat spoon of mashed potatoes onto each plate, she helped Shanon fit the dishes nicely. Shanon was amazed. None of the little hens even touched.

"Thanks, Mrs. Bu—I mean, Mrs. Worth!" she said gratefully.

The English cook smiled knowingly as Shanon shot through the door. Mrs. Worth knew the girls called her Mrs. Butter behind her back, and it actually pleased her. Nicknames are a form of endearment, she thought, and the name they'd chosen for her was both appropriate and clever. The roly-poly Englishwoman was as soft and sweet as Mrs. Butterworth's pancake syrup.

"Here's the entree!" Shanon announced, hurrying toward the table. "Sorry I'm so behind! I'll make sure that you get your dessert—"

"Look!" Coach Barker exclaimed. "My favorite! Rock Cornish—"

A sudden crash echoed through the dining hall. Shanon never knew how it happened. Everyone's eyes turned to the floor. There amidst the mashed potatoes and smashed china sat seven game hens!

Coach Barker was the first to start laughing. "I'm sorry," she guffawed, her eyes watering. "I've just never seen so many little chickens on the floor before."

"It does look funny," Brenda joined in, giggling.

Soon everyone else at the table was laughing, and then the laughter spread through the whole dining hall. It was too awful not to be funny. Somebody at another table clinked a glass and shouted: "Encore! Hooray for the waitress and her flying game hens!"

Shanon's eyes filled with tears as she stood above the ruined dinners. But then she caught Amy's sympathetic smile, and suddenly Shanon began to laugh, too.

"Sorry," she announced, blushing. "I guess I've got butter fingers."

"It's okay," Lisa said, jumping up to help her. Palmer and Amy got up to help, too.

"I never did like these silly little hens, anyway," Palmer drawled, giving Shanon a comforting pat.

"I'll go get some more," Shanon said, lifting the tray full of hens and broken dishes.

"Take your time," Amy encouraged.

"Don't be so nervous," Lisa said, smiling.

"I won't be if you and Palmer stop fighting," Shanon said, moving off swiftly.

Lisa sat down again, not feeling nearly so mad as before. She was sorry that her bad temper had made Shanon so jumpy.

"Well, this meal started off with a bang," Coach Barker spoke up good-naturedly. Then she turned to Lisa. "I hope to see you at tryouts."

Lisa gulped. "Me?"

"I heard that you were interested in the tennis team," the coach prompted.

Palmer gave Lisa a dirty look, then changed her expression when she saw Shanon appear with fresh entrees. Within minutes the whole table had been served and everyone was digging into the delicious food.

"You're a very good player," the coach continued.

"Thank you," Lisa said uneasily. "But I'm not interested in going out for the tennis team."

"Too bad," the coach said. "We could use some fresh blood."

Lisa picked at her meal thoughtfully. "I don't know where you got the idea that I would go out for tennis, but if you're looking for new talent, I know a very good player."

"Who is it?" the coach asked.

"She's sitting right here at the table," Lisa announced proudly. "It's Palmer Durand."

Amy grinned happily, but Palmer looked down in embarrassment. If the coach had been interested in her for the team, she would have said something that afternoon . . . wouldn't she?

"Durand, is that true?" the coach asked in a friendly voice. "I've heard about your mother, of course. She's a legend here. But from what you said earlier, I didn't think you wanted to compete in the sport."

"Well, I've been out practicing every day," Palmer said.

"I've seen you," the coach said. "But I thought you were just training McGreevy."

Palmer looked pleased. "Me? Training Lisa?"

"It was the other way around," Lisa corrected her. "Palmer didn't want to approach you until her form was perfected. She's been out of practice."

36

"That's right!" Palmer jumped in.

"Well, in that case," said Barker, "why don't you come and talk with me tomorrow at the gym. Maybe we can get you into the round robin."

"That's the main reason I'm interested," Palmer blurted out.

Mr. Griffith's green eyes twinkled as Shanon brought them their apple pie. He glanced across the room at Miss Grayson, and the pretty French teacher smiled and waved. "Now we're a happy group," he enthused. "And why shouldn't we be? It's spring!"

"That was quite a tumble you took with those hens, Shanon," Mrs. Worth said, dipping her hands into the dough she was working. The cook had asked Shanon to stay after supper and help her make pastry. "Now tell me what's on your mind."

Shanon paused, wondering whether to confide in the Englishwoman. Mrs. Worth was almost always warm and friendly, but she was so much older. And she could be stern sometimes, too. She seemed like a combination of the Queen of Hearts in *Alice in Wonderland* and Shanon's very favorite aunt, who lived in Boston.

"There's a problem in our suite," Shanon began, deciding to trust her.

The cook kept her eyes on the dough. "What kind?"

"I guess you could say it's about boys," Shanon replied. "It's taken over our suite."

"We all have boy problems at one time or another," the cook said, nodding. "What's yours about?"

"Oh, I don't have one," Shanon explained. "I *am* worried about this boy who's my pen pal and hasn't written in a while. But the main problem is with the other girls in the suite, especially my roommate. She can't think about anything but this boy."

"Poor dear," Mrs. Butter said, punching the dough. "She'll have to learn a big word, I'm afraid."

"What word?" Shanon asked, puzzled.

Mrs. Butter sat down and grinned. Her hands were covered with flour. "Priorities," she said, shaking her head.

Shanon's eyebrows rose. "What do you mean?"

"Sit down," Mrs. Butter offered. She wiped her hands and put on some tea. "Let's chat a bit. . . ."

By the time Shanon got back to Fox Hall, it was after lights-out. The sitting room was dark, but she could hear Lisa's giggle coming from Amy and Palmer's room.

"What's going on?" she whispered, creeping in.

"We're having a discussion," Amy said. "Come on in."

The other three Foxes were on the floor, drinking sodas. Moonlight flooded in through the window above them, and their faces and nightgowns shone in the silvery light.

"Coach Barker asked me to go out for the tennis team," Palmer announced, smiling.

Shanon took a deep breath. "I'm glad for you. But we've got to talk about some things. Like priorities."

Lisa giggled. "We all know what our priorities are."

"No, you don't!" Shanon objected, trying to keep her voice down. "Mrs. Butter and I had a good talk. I told her

38

how we've been on each other's backs and all because of a bunch of boys, and she gave me some important advice. She said—"

Lisa tugged at Shanon's hand. "Hold on. We're not mad at each other anymore. You don't have to be upset."

"Relax and take off your jacket," Amy encouraged.

"Not until I get this off my chest," insisted Shanon. She crouched down in front of them. "If this pen pals business is going to take over our lives, I'd rather just drop the whole thing," she announced.

For a moment, everyone was quiet.

"I guess I *have* gotten a little carried away about Rob," Lisa admitted. "I apologize for making it everyone's problem."

"It *is* our problem if you're going nuts," Shanon said. "What you have to decide is what's most important— that's how Mrs. Butter put it, and I know she's right."

"We've been talking about just that," Amy said, nodding her head. "Lisa and Palmer had a really big fight because of this misunderstanding about Lisa going out for the tennis team."

"And Palmer never would have been so upset about it if she wasn't so concerned about playing with Simmie," Lisa added.

"That's right," Amy agreed. "Palmer jumped to the wrong conclusion."

"Not exactly," Shanon said. "One day when Coach Barker was watching the two of you practice, I accidentally gave her the wrong impression. So it was really my fault."

"Oh, yes. I remember now," Amy chimed in. "But *I* wasn't even sure who the coach was watching. It was just an honest misunderstanding."

There was a moment of relieved silence.

"So much for boy craziness, huh?" Shanon said.

"No more craziness," Lisa repeated, giggling. "I can't promise no more boys though!"

"Nobody's asking you to do that," Amy teased. "We'd just appreciate it if you could think about something else at the same time."

"Like your roommate," Shanon said, "and your history paper."

"I've been neglecting my photography project, too," Lisa said thoughtfully.

"Above all," Amy declared, "*we're* what's most important. The Foxes! We live with each other."

"That's right," Shanon added. "If we gave up pen pals, we would still be the Foxes. Wouldn't we?"

"Of course we would," Lisa assured her. "That's not just our code name. That's *us!*"

Amy slapped her hand down in the middle of their circle. Lisa put her hand on top, then Shanon added hers, and they all looked at Palmer.

"Okay," Palmer murmured, resting her hand on the pile. "No more boys on the brain. From now on, the only thing on my mind is playing tennis." She lowered her eyes and smiled slyly. Day and night she would only think about tennis . . . tennis with Simmie Randolph III.

CHAPTER FIVE

Dear Rob,

For your information, Pennsylvania is not boring. In the town where I live there is a genuine ferris-wheel factory, a shop where chocolate is made and given away free, and an old cemetery where the people died hundreds of years ago and you can do rubbings. Our drive-in movie theater has the Rocky Horror Show every midnight, and I can get in for FREE.

Don't think that by saying all this, I am trying to talk you out of going to Alaska. I'm sure that will be interesting in other ways, especially if you like musk ox better than people. Though I'll be living in Pennsylvania this summer, I would have been too busy to see you even if you had decided to work there.

This summer I will probably continue to work on my photography project. I have been taking pictures of found objects and developing them. Sometimes they are like an optical illusion. For example, the other day I found an old umbrella out on the street near the quad. It was all crushed and mangled. I think the za-wagon (that's what we call Figaro Pizza's delivery van) must have run over it. But in the picture I took, it didn't look just like an umbrella. Do you know what it looked like? A STINKING, ROTTEN DEAD BAT! Maybe I should send you a copy of it. I have to close now as I am very busy.

Yours truly,
Lisa McGreevy

Dear Lisa,

Are you mad about something? I hope that you are planning to send me a picture of a dead bat and not the real thing. I also hope that you are not too busy to write again. Please explain.

Rob Williams

Dear Mars,

I have already written to you twice and you haven't answered. Please tell me how you are and what you are doing. Do you have a problem?

Sincerely,
Shanon

Dear Shanon,

I apologize for not writing in a while. I do have a problem, but no one can help.

Mars

Dear John,

Did you get my letter? I wrote to you about your poem and I was honest. How's the weather down there? Up here on the mountain, it's soggy. Wish we could write another song together. I still appreciate how much you helped me out on my song "Cabin Fever."

Yours truly,
Amy

Dear Amy,

Number one: I did not write you because I think you were way out of line trashing my poem like that. What do you know about poetry anyway?

Number two: "Cabin Fever" is not just your song, it's mine too since I contributed a lot to the lyrics!

Number three: My poem is not offensive to women. If you understood it, you would know that.

Number four: I'm just being honest.

Yours truly,
John Adams

P.S. Now I see why Alma and Ardsley never have classes together. They couldn't—men and women don't have the same sort of intelligence.

"Of all the nerve!" Amy exclaimed, storming through the room. She tore off her skirt and blouse and went for her jogging clothes. "I have to go run or I'm going to explode."

"Don't explode," Lisa said slyly. "Remember what you

43

told me—there are more important things on this earth than our pen pals."

"Yes. We weren't going to get all excited about boy problems," Shanon reminded her.

"This isn't about boy problems!" Amy sputtered. "This is about a principle! This is a free country—I have a right to my opinion about what I read, including John's poetry!"

"It sounds like you hurt his feelings," Lisa surmised.

"Too bad!" Amy countered. "He asked me to be brutally honest, but now he can't take it!"

"He asked you to be honest," Shanon corrected her. "I don't remember anything about the brutal part."

"Maybe you weren't sensitive enough in your criticism," Lisa suggested.

Amy flushed with embarrassment. Maybe Lisa had a point, but Amy wasn't about to back down. "John wasn't sensitive either," she said stubbornly. "His poem is clearly insulting to girls. And so is this crack in his letter about men and women having different kinds of intelligence!" She snatched a tape off the bureau and put it in her Walkman. "I need music! Maybe you were right, Shanon. Maybe we should just end pen pals!"

"I said we should do that only if writing to the boys took over our lives," Shanon reminded her.

"And pen pals is not taking over *my* life anymore," Lisa declared. "I'm keeping my mind on photography."

"I'm not surprised," Shanon said, lifting an eyebrow. "After the mean letter you wrote Rob, I wouldn't be looking forward to his answer either."

Lisa smiled wryly. "Do you think my letter was mean?"

"You know it was," said Shanon.

"How else was I going to put him out of my mind?" Lisa protested. "If he doesn't like me well enough to want to be near me this summer, then I don't like him either!"

"But you *do* like him," Shanon insisted. "I think it would have been better if you'd just told him that."

"Tell Rob Williams that I like him?" Lisa sounded shocked. "I couldn't! Not in a thousand years."

"At least tell him that you're disappointed he's not working in Pennsylvania," Amy suggested. "Be honest."

"Why should I?" argued Lisa. "Look where honesty got you!"

Amy turned toward the window. "Rats!" she muttered. "Looks like another downpour. I wish this weather would make up its mind."

"Maybe you shouldn't go running," Lisa said, handing Shanon some of her latest pictures. "What do you think of these?"

Shanon leafed through the stack. Lisa's black and white photographs were all of found objects—a stick that looked like a snake, a tree fungus that could have been a sea shell, a feather that resembled a comb. Shanon smiled wistfully. "They're wonderful. They all look so lonely though."

"Give me a break," Amy groaned. "Since when is tree fungus lonely?"

"Sorry." Shanon shrugged as she gave the pictures back. "I'm in a sad mood, I suppose. Just thinking about Mars."

"I wonder what his problem is," Lisa said.

"Maybe he's having trouble with his grades," Amy offered.

"It would have to be worse than that to get Mars down," Shanon replied.

"I hope it's nothing serious, like his parents getting a divorce," Lisa said.

"Whatever it is," Shanon sighed, "I wish he would tell me."

Thunder crashed outside the window. "There goes my breath of fresh air!" Amy moaned, throwing herself onto the floor. "Guess I'll do some push-ups."

"I'll put on some music," Lisa volunteered, reaching for a Grateful Dead CD. "You know what's the most depressing thing of all?" she yelled over the music.

"What?" Amy grunted, already doing her exercise.

"There's a dance at Ardsley coming up in a few weeks, and not one of The Unknown has invited us."

"And the way things are going," Shanon said, looking up from her French, "probably none of them will."

Lisa sat up and turned the music off. "What a bummer! And that was the main reason we advertised for pen pals— so we could have dates. Now look what's happened to us. Writing to them is more complicated than having real boyfriends."

"Don't worry," Amy said, flipping onto her back for some sit-ups, "my mother always says that the sun is just behind the rain clouds. Something really good is going to happen any minute."

Just then Palmer burst into the suite. Her golden hair

was dripping wet, and so was her tennis sweater. "I've got the greatest news," she said, smiling broadly.

The other girls looked at her. For a moment they were dumbfounded. Was this Palmer, soaked to the skin and not a word of complaint?

"What's happened?" Amy asked. "Besides being caught in a thunderstorm!"

"Everything!" Palmer exclaimed. "I finished my tryout, and I've just been to see Coach Barker—"

"And?" Lisa cut in eagerly.

"And I made the team!" Palmer announced. "She says that I'm the best player to come around in years. She called me a prod—prodi—"

"A prodigy?" Shanon helped out.

"Yes," Palmer replied. "I'm a tennis genius."

"Yippee!" Amy yelled. "You probably inherited it from your mother."

"All those summers at tennis camp didn't hurt, either," Palmer said. "But without Lisa's training I wouldn't have made it."

Lisa looked at Palmer and was amazed to see real gratitude in her eyes. "Thanks," Lisa said modestly. "But you're the one who did the work. Sorry I was such a grouchy coach."

"You had a right to be grouchy," Palmer admitted.

"This round robin is going to be some event," Amy exclaimed. "And one of the Foxes is going to be in it!"

"We'll all have to go," Shanon said. "To watch Palmer."

47

Palmer blushed and smiled. And just for one moment, she forgot all about Simmie.

Dear Rob,

As you see, I am not too busy to keep writing to you. And I am not mad about anything at all. Honest. I just thought you would like Pennsylvania.

Yesterday I shot a whole roll of film down by the river. Have you ever noticed how amazing rocks look under water? I also took another picture of a found object—this time someone's wasted gym sock. In the mud it looked just like what it was, a gym sock!

Yours truly,
Lisa

P.S. Hope my previous letter wasn't mean.
P.P.S. My suitemate Palmer is going to be in the round robin tournament. I hear some of the Ardsley guys are coming over. How about The Unknown?

Dear John,

Number one: Men and women do not have different kinds of intelligence as far as I know. Unless you mean to say that women are smarter. And though I don't know that much about poetry, I gave you a gut reaction to what you had written. A gut reaction, in my opinion, is the highest form of intelligence.

Number two: I found that your poem was insulting to girls because you implied that girls can't play ball or climb mountains and that you wanted them to leave you alone.

Number three: "Cabin Fever" is my song.
Number four: I'm sorry I was insensitive.

Yours truly,
Amy

P.S. Are you coming to watch the tennis round robin? I hear that Simmie is playing. So is Palmer. It would be nice to see you.

Dear Simmie,
I am so excited about the round robin—I can hardly wait! Coach Barker says I'm in shape!

Yours truly,
Palmer

CHAPTER SIX

"What year was the Battle of Hastings?" Shanon quizzed. Dressed in a yellow slicker and black boots, she looked like a fire fighter. Lisa trudged alongside her in an old green cape, while Amy and Palmer walked a few feet behind. Amy wore a black derby and pullover sweater, and Palmer looked as stylish as ever in a new trenchcoat with matching umbrella.

"Come on, everybody," Shanon prodded. "Mr. Seganish is definitely going to ask us this date on the history quiz."

"Ten sixty-six!" Palmer piped up.

"That's right," Shanon said.

Amy grinned. "Look who's been studying!"

"I have to get a decent grade this time," Palmer announced, "in order to stay on the team."

"I've got to get a decent grade, too," Lisa grumbled. "My father's been checking up on me. But I feel totally unprepared for this morning's quiz."

"That's because you've been in the darkroom every day this week," Shanon reminded her.

"My photography project is important," Lisa said.

"My staying on the tennis team is important, too," Palmer boasted, "but I still find time for my studies."

"That's only because you're desperate to be in the round robin with Simmie Randolph," Lisa said, feeling irked. She was pleased her suitemate was doing so well—she just wished Palmer didn't always have to look so pleased with herself. "Simmie is the only reason you're even interested in tennis."

"Stop bugging her!" Amy cut in. "And anyway, it's not true. Palmer is into tennis because she gets something out of it. Just like I get something out of playing soccer and softball. Right, Palmer?"

"Yes . . . that's true," Palmer said hesitantly. She hadn't thought about it before, but Amy *was* right. She enjoyed being on the team. In fact, if Simmie decided not to play in the round robin, she'd probably still want to be involved in it.

Mr. Seganish was passing out the quizzes by the time the Foxes got to class. The history teacher was over six feet tall, had a bald head, and was fond of telling stories. In fact, Seganish's storytelling ability was well known and accounted for history being one of Lisa's favorite classes. When Seganish started telling anecdotes about some historical place or person, he got so absorbed in what he was saying that the students in the class could do just about anything—as long as they were discreet about it. Lisa found history class a good place to write letters. She rarely looked up at the teacher unless he cracked a pun or bad joke, both of which he was also well known for.

But today Lisa wished she were anywhere but history class. Seganish wasn't talking, and there was a quiz to take. To top it off, the classroom was stuffy, making Lisa's blurry memory of the facts and dates she'd barely studied even blurrier.

Palmer, on the other hand, was well prepared for the first time ever. The hundreds of facts she'd crammed into her brain the night before were still fresh. Luckily, the quiz was multiple choice—an essay would have been a lot harder. Of course she had no idea why it was so important to know that the Battle of Hastings took place in 1066, but if it would help her stay on the tennis team, she was determined to remember it. She finished the quiz with a minute to spare. Shanon and Amy, who were both excellent students, had finished some time before. But over by the closed window, Lisa was still struggling.

"That's it!" Mr. Seganish suddenly announced. He smiled in Palmer's direction. "Might I have your exam, please, Miss Durand?"

Palmer was pleasantly embarrassed. Seganish had never smiled at her before. She had always been one of his worst students.

"Coach Barker tells me you're a talent on the tennis court," the teacher said as Palmer handed over her test. "The round robin is a great favorite of mine. Miss Grayson and I will be sitting out in the bleachers."

52

Palmer's eyes widened. She'd forgotten that the entire faculty would be in the audience.

"That is," Mr. Seganish added with a chortle, "we will if those old bleachers hold us up. Otherwise, we'll be sitting on our seats! Ha, ha. Then I guess Miss Pryn will have to order some new benches out there by the courts."

Palmer knew Seganish had tried to make a joke. She didn't get it, but she laughed politely anyway. As she got up, she saw that Lisa, Shanon, and Amy were waiting at the door for her.

"Am I glad to get out of there!" Lisa said, taking a deep breath once they were in the hallway. "Somebody ought to tell him to get some fresh air in there."

"Somebody ought to tell him about his jokes," Amy giggled.

"Did you hear what he said about coming to the round robin with Miss Grayson?" Shanon whispered. "I wonder if that means that they're dating each other."

Lisa shook her head. "Poor Mr. Griffith! It's obvious he likes Miss Grayson. Why would she want to go anywhere with Mr. Seganish? He's nowhere near as handsome as Mr. Griffith!"

Amy shrugged. "Maybe she had an argument with Mr. Griffith, and Mr. Seganish is being nice to her."

"Mr. Seganish *is* very nice," Palmer agreed. "He's coming to the round robin just to see me play."

Shanon smiled. "I suppose a lot of people will be there. Are you nervous?"

"I can handle it," Palmer replied nonchalantly. Actually,

53

as the round robin got closer and closer, she was growing more worried. There were a lot of pressures to deal with. She had to play well—Simmie would be there! Coach Barker had put a lot of faith in her. And now that she knew the other teachers would be coming, too . . .

Amy threw an arm over Palmer's shoulder. "Don't anybody worry about my roomie being nervous!" she warned. "She can handle anything!"

Palmer glowed. Amy actually sounded proud to be her roommate! She wondered if her mom would be proud of her, too. When she and Simmie won the round robin, Palmer decided, she would write her mother a long letter. Since she'd come to Alma, she'd only written a few short notes.

"I'm going to the *Ledger* office," Shanon announced.

"I'm going to the bathroom to put on some lipstick," Lisa said.

"Not too much," Amy said with a laugh. "Kate'll report you!" She hooked Palmer's elbow. "Going over to the gym?"

Palmer nodded.

"I'll come with you," Amy said. "Softball practice has been hard on my pitching arm. I need the whirlpool."

The Foxes parted ways.

Outside it was still drizzling, as Shanon hurried to the *Ledger* office. When she got there, Kate was at her desk with the drawer open.

"You scared me!" Kate burst out in a startled voice. "I thought you were Dolores!"

"Why don't you want to see Dolores?" Shanon asked, shrugging out of her slicker and hanging it up.

Kate opened the drawer to her desk a little wider. "I've got Tickle in here!" she whispered conspiratorially.

"You still have that kitten?" Shanon asked in a whisper.

"I haven't found a home for her yet," Kate said. She lifted the calico cat out of the drawer and cuddled her.

"Why didn't you leave Tickle in your room? That would be safer."

"I haven't got the heart," Kate confessed. "I leave my room so early. She's by herself all day. Besides, she meows. Somebody might hear her."

"But what are you going to do if Dolores comes into the office?" Shanon exclaimed.

"I'll hide her," Kate replied.

Shanon shook her head. "If you hide that kitten in your desk, Dolores is definitely going to hear her and turn you in. Then they'll take Tickle away, and you'll get in trouble."

"I'm not letting anybody take Tickle!" Kate said, straightening her glasses defiantly. "The rule about no pets is unfair! I'll be a test case. Miss Pryn will have to suspend me."

Shanon looked at her watch. "At one o'clock I'm going on the computer with the Journalism Club. Want to join me?"

"Not today," Kate said. Dressing to go outdoors, she tucked Tickle under her raincoat. "All this talk about having to give Tickle away has made me very nervous. It's not safe for her here. I'll have to find some other hiding place."

Kate walked out, and Shanon turned on the computer. The Journalism Club would meet in one minute. There was nothing Shanon particularly wanted to discuss today, but she was hoping that the Ardsley Lit. Mag. would be online. Maybe then she could confer with Amy's pen pal, John Adams.

By keying in *The Ledger*'s ID number and password, she put herself in touch with several other junior and senior high school journalists. This afternoon's topic was how to do research for an article, and the students were sharing information. As the club members identified themselves, Shanon was happy to note that John was among them. She waited for an opportunity to shoot over a message.

THIS IS SHANON DAVIS, STEPHENS LEDGER. I SHARED THE INFO ON HOW I RESEARCHED MY ARTICLE ON LIFE IN GIRLS SCHOOLS AT AN EARLIER MEETING; HOWEVER WHEN THE CLUB IS ADJOURNED WOULD LIKE TO MEET ARDSLEY LIT. MAG. IN A CONFERENCE ROOM.

A reply from John flashed on the screen.

OKAY, SHANON. MEET YOU WHEN THE MEETING IS OVER. BY THE WAY, DO YOU KNOW THE OKAY AND GA SYMBOLS IN COMPUTER LANGUAGE? OKAY INDICATES THAT I HAVE RECEIVED YOUR MESSAGE. GA INDICATES THAT YOU CAN GO AHEAD. IN OTHER WORDS I'M READY TO RECEIVE YOU. JOHN ADAMS./GA

OKAY, OKAY, JOHN. WHO DO YOU THINK

YOU'RE TALKING TO? OF COURSE I KNOW THE SYMBOLS! DO YOU THINK THAT GIRLS WOULDN'T BE FAMILIAR WITH THAT KIND OF THING?/GA

OKAY, TOUCHE SHANON! I SEE THAT YOU'VE BEEN TALKING TO AMY HO ABOUT MY BEING A CHAUVINIST. DIDN'T MEAN TO INSULT YOUR FEMININE ABILITIES./GA

OKAY, JOHN. LET'S SAVE THIS UNTIL LATER.

Shanon knew that time on the computer was supposed to be reserved for journalism matters. But she and John had spoken privately before during another emergency. Then it had been about John and Amy; this time it was about her and Mars.

When the meeting was over and the other journalists had exited the Club, John and Shanon got back online.

OKAY, SHANON. WHAT DO YOU WANT TO TALK ABOUT?/GA

OKAY, JOHN. SORRY I WAS SO TOUCHY BEFORE. THIS IS IMPORTANT AND QUITE PERSONAL./GA

OKAY, SHANON. SOUNDS JUICY. BUT MAKE IT QUICK. I ALMOST GOT CAUGHT DOING THIS LAST TIME./GA

OKAY. I AM WORRIED ABOUT MY PEN PAL MARS. HOW IS HE?/GA

OKAY, MARS IS VERY DOWN THESE DAYS. HE IS NOT HIS ZANY SELF. HE'S NOT THINKING UP SCHEMES. HE IS NO LONGER JOKING. HE IS MISSING CLASS./GA

OKAY, UNKNOWN. DO YOU KNOW WHY?/GA

OKAY, FOX, WE ARE IN THE DARK. MARS
DOESN'T WANT TO TALK ABOUT IT. WE THINK IT
IS A FAMILY PROBLEM./GA

OKAY, ARE HIS PARENTS GETTING A DIVORCE?
/GA

OKAY, WE ARE NOT SURE. ANYWAY IF MARS
WANTED TO TELL ANYBODY, HE WOULD. A MAN
HAS A RIGHT TO HIS PRIVACY./GA

OKAY, EVEN IF HE IS DEPRESSED? MARS IS MY
FRIEND. MAYBE I CAN HELP./GA

OKAY, SHANON,I DOUBT IT AND I HAVE TO GO.
CAN'T SPEND ANYMORE OF THE MAG.'S MONEY
LIKE THIS. TELL AMY THAT I AM NOT A CHAU-
VINIST AND THAT I WILL BE AT THE ROUND
ROBIN./GA

OKAY, IS MARS COMING TOO?/GA

OKAY, FOX,I'LL TRY TO GET HIM THERE./GA

OKAY, UNKNOWN. THANKS FOR YOUR HELP.
/GA

OKAY, GOOD-BYE. SAY HI TO AMY./GA

"I talked to John over the computer today," Shanon told
Lisa in their room that evening. "He thinks Mars has a
family problem."

Lisa yawned and scratched her head. "Too bad. You
can't do anything about that."

"I guess not," Shanon said.

"I can't believe how tired I am," Lisa sighed. "And I still
have to go over my Latin vocabulary."

Shanon shifted in bed. Her quilt was covered with pieces

58

of notebook paper. She was working on an essay for Mr. Griffith's class. "Do you think it would be better if Alma was co-ed?" she asked thoughtfully.

"I used to," Lisa replied, "but not anymore."

"You once said you'd want to be anyplace in the world with Rob," Shanon reminded her.

"I changed my mind," Lisa said. "It would be too dangerous to be with Rob every day. Instead of writing him a mean letter, I probably would scream at him for not working in Pennsylvania. Then instead of just not liking me, he'd hate me. And anyway, the clothes we have to wear to class are too dull-looking. I wouldn't want Rob to see me dressed like that all the time."

Shanon picked up the picture of Mars she kept on the nightstand. His face was so interesting and friendly. And she liked the dark cowlick in the front of his hair. "I sure wish I went to class with Mars," she said.

"Why?" Lisa asked, giggling wickedly. "So he could hold your hand?"

Shanon smiled. "That would be nice, but it wasn't what I was thinking." She stared at the picture. "If Mars were here right now, all I'd want to do . . . is talk."

CHAPTER SEVEN

The day of the round robin, the sky was filled with fluffy clouds. Palmer woke up, then dressed carefully in a brand new white tennis outfit with light blue trim. She brushed her hair until it glistened and fastened it back with a new blue clip in the shape of a flower. Then she lightly applied some pale pink lipstick. *I look wonderful!* she thought, standing away from the mirror. *I look almost like an athlete!* From the hours of practice, her body was tan and looked more muscular.

"What time is it?" Amy grumbled, shifting under her covers. "It must be dawn. Why are you up?"

"Mrs. Butter is giving me an early breakfast," Palmer explained, "and then I want to warm up a little. Today's the round robin—remember?"

"I remember," Amy replied, yawning. "Good luck! We'll be in the stands, watching your every move. Now, let me go back to sleep."

Palmer smiled as her roommate burrowed back under

the covers. Amy had been absolutely great about everything lately. Even Lisa seemed to be on Palmer's side these
days. And Shanon was always so nice and encouraging! It
wasn't just for herself that Palmer wanted to do well in the
round robin—it was for the other Foxes, too. She wanted
to make them proud. And, of course, she wanted to play
well for Simmie!

Down by the courts two hours later, Palmer waited
breathlessly for the Ardsley buses to arrive. By this time she
was so nervous she could hardly stand still. Coach Barker
had paired her with a fifth-former named Megan Morgan
for a warm-up. Megan was regarded as Alma's best player,
and Palmer liked her a lot. Since Palmer had joined the
team, Megan had been like a big sister.

"Do well out there today, Durand," Megan encouraged,
as she stretched her leg against the back fence of the court.

"I will," Palmer grinned, practicing her swing. "Watch
out, we might be playing against each other."

"I'm counting on it," Megan said. "I don't know what
the coaches have planned, but we'll probably all come up
against each other at some point during the day. I just hope
I get some good partners from Ardsley."

"My partner is going to be the best player they've got,"
Palmer boasted. "At least in the beginning. I'm going to be
paired with my boyfriend for the first match."

Megan looked impressed. "Wow . . . that's an advan-
tage. The two of you must have had a lot of practice
playing together."

"Not really," Palmer replied. She was about to explain

61

to Megan that Simmie wasn't actually her boyfriend yet but only her pen pal when the Ardsley buses rolled into the parking lot. Palmer spotted them and ran to the fence. "There they are!"

"Off the court, ladies," Coach Barker instructed. "Let's give the gentlemen some space for their warm-up."

Palmer lagged behind, trying to get a glimpse of Simmie. From a distance she saw his amazingly thick blonde hair, as he emerged from the bus. He was dressed all in white, naturally, except for a blue sweat band. Palmer's heart pounded—it was all happening just as she'd imagined!

"Go sit in the shade, Durand," the coach commanded. "Haven't you ever seen boys before?"

"Sure," Palmer replied, a little embarrassed, as she turned to find a seat.

The Alma team sat in the shade along the sideline, as the boys approached at the other end of the courts. Palmer's eyes found and followed Simmie. He hadn't waved hello to her yet. She wondered if he had seen her.

"A few words before we start," Coach Barker began, standing in front of the group.

Palmer leaned forward. The coach was blocking her vision.

"Number one—" Barker said, "have fun out there. A round robin is a chance to see how you can adapt to the styles of other players, a chance to improvise. Not only that, it's a chance to compete with the best—one another!"

The coach moved out of the way, and Simmie appeared in Palmer's line of vision. They caught eyes for a moment, and he waved at her. Flushing with pleasure, she waved back. The coach was finishing her pep talk. "And finally, above all," Barker said, "keep your mind and eye on the ball. . . ."

"I'm going to faint this minute," Lisa whispered.

"Pull yourself together," Amy cautioned, trying to hide how shaky she herself felt. John, Rob, and Mars had gotten off the bus several minutes earlier. At first they seemed to be heading toward the clump of trees where the girls were standing. But then they'd suddenly stopped and formed a huddle.

"I'm glad Mars came at least," Shanon said, furrowing her brow. "I hope he talks to me."

"Why are they just standing there?" Lisa whispered. "Suppose they decide not to sit with us! Rob's letters have been so weird lately."

"Things have been weird with me and John, too," Amy said.

"How do we look?" Shanon asked nervously. Hoping the round robin wasn't considered an official function, the Foxes had gone off the dress code. Shanon was wearing a pair of green shorts and a matching top she'd gotten from Palmer. Her wavy hair was tied back with a bow. Lisa had on the red and black toreadors, a white cotton sweater and dangling earrings. Amy was wearing black stretch pants, a while tuxedo shirt and a leather vest. Her hair was moussed and her jet black eyes were lined with kohl.

"We look *fine*," Lisa said. The thought that The Unknowns might actually be about to ignore them was already making her angry. "Look at the way *they're* dressed!" The Foxes gazed at the boys' backs as they remained in a huddle. The Unknowns were wearing jeans and nondescript T-shirts. But when they turned back around in the girls' direction again, all three had put on mirrored glasses.

"Here they come," Shanon said excitedly.

The girls stared. The boys were as good-looking as ever. Tall, dark-haired Rob finally approached Lisa. "Hey, what's up?" he said awkwardly. "We thought you girls might save us a seat."

"We weren't sure you were coming," Lisa replied, trying to sound casual. Seeing her reflection in Rob's glasses was distracting.

"At least we thought you'd come over and say hello," John Adams put in. Amy's tall, redheaded pen pal squared off with her.

"Why didn't you say hello to us?" Amy said, staring defiantly at John's mirrored glasses. With his eyes covered, how could she really know what he was thinking?

"That would have been too chauvinistic," John replied with a wry smile.

Shanon smiled at Mars. "I'm glad to see you."

"I'm glad to see you, too," he said quietly. Shanon thought he looked unhappy. If only she could do something about it!

The three couples stared at each other and then stared at the ground.

"It's a good thing you're *supposed* to be quiet during a tennis match," Lisa giggled uncomfortably.

Rob grabbed Lisa's hand, dropped it like a hot potato,

and then quickly picked it up again. "Excuse me," he muttered, getting flustered. "That is . . . let's take seats, shall we?"

Meanwhile, down on the courts, Simmie and Palmer had met at the sideline.

"So, it's finally happening," Palmer said breathlessly. Simmie's green eyes glinted in the sunlight. They were such a blinding color she could hardly look into them.

He flashed a big smile. "Just you and me and a hundred people watching us," he said smoothly. "Maybe after this is over, we can find someplace to chat by ourselves. I have something to tell you."

"About the dance?" Palmer gasped, catching her breath.

Simmie's tan face turned beet red. "Yes," he said. "How did you know?"

Palmer smiled. Of course Simmie would be inviting her to the dance. She'd always known he would, just like she knew they'd win the round robin together.

Coach Barker's voice rang out over the loudspeaker:

"As a courtesy to the players, we ask that the audience hold its applause until the end of a point." Then she read off the names of the first-round partners. "On court number one, Palmer Durand from Alma Stephens and Simmie Randolph the Third from Ardsley Academy."

Palmer's heart skipped a beat. It was just as Simmie had promised! In the first round they were playing against Brenda Smith and a guy from Ardsley named Gary Hawkins. Brenda was a pretty average player, and Gary Hawkins had too nice a face to be ruthless. Judging from the way Simmie's face was set as he swaggered onto the court,

Palmer guessed he would play very aggressively. *We've got it made!* she thought, sizing up the competition.

Palmer and Simmie were magic together. While Simmie, quick and catlike, guarded the net, Palmer was steady as a machine, slamming returns from the base line. Cheers rose from the crowd with the final point. Palmer couldn't believe she and Simmie had won their first match.

Shifting to another court, Palmer was paired with Gary Hawkins and then later with another boy. Each time she and her Ardsley partner won their match. Palmer even won when Megan Morgan was playing against her. Glancing downcourt, she saw that Simmie seemed to be doing well in his matches also. And then they were paired again—this time against Megan and Gary Hawkins.

"Let's get them, babe," Simmie whispered.

Palmer smiled.

"I hate to lose," he added, with his jaw tightening.

"We're going to win," she shot back.

Palmer had never had such an amazing experience. Not only was she competing, she was coming out on top. And what a thrill it was to be with a player as powerful as Simmie. But even though Palmer and Simmie continued to play well, this time their opponents played even better. Megan and Gary were the winners!

"What happened to you?" Simmie snarled as he and Palmer walked off the court.

"I did the best I could," Palmer said with hurt feelings.

"Do better the next time," he ordered. "I told you I don't like losing."

The players took a break. In a moment, the coaches

would name the teams for the special exhibition match—the two top girls and two top boys. Palmer took a gulp from her water bottle and tried to catch Simmie's eye.

"Sorry I was rough on you," he said, coming over. "But I don't like anything to stand in the way of my winning. Right now I could kill that Hawkins guy. Whenever I lose, I really hate the person who beats me."

Palmer looked at him with a mixture of awe and bewilderment. It never occurred to her that anyone would take a game so seriously.

"Killer instinct is part of being a winner," Simmer added boastfully just before Coach Barker's voice came over the loudspeaker:

"For your enjoyment," she announced, "we have selected two teams from among the groups for a mixed-doubles play-off. From Alma Stephens, Megan Morgan and Palmer Durand. From Ardsley Academy, Simmie Randolph and Gary Hawkins. Megan will be partnered with Simmie, and Palmer with Gary."

Palmer's blue eyes flew open. *There must be a mistake!* she thought, glancing around wildly. She watched Simmie walk away with Megan as Gary came toward her. Her hands began to shake. This couldn't be right. She was supposed to be playing *with* Simmie, not *against* him!

Gary Hawkins walked up to her and smiled. "I've been admiring your game," he said in a friendly voice. "You've got a terrific backhand."

Palmer took her position and glanced across the net at Megan and Simmie. Megan's face was all concentration, but Simmie was glaring at her.

In the audience, the Foxes and their pen pals exchanged comments.

"Look at Palmer!" Lisa whispered. "Doesn't she look incredible?"

"She's playing better than I ever thought she could," Amy whispered back.

"Yeah, but now she's matched up against Randolph," Rob muttered.

"Hawkins is a good player, too," John volunteered. "This should be interesting."

Shanon nudged Mars gently. He seemed to be a thousand miles away. "Enjoying yourself?"

"Yes, it's a good exhibition," he said tonelessly.

The one-set exhibition match was breathtaking. Megan Morgan was in top form and Palmer, inspired by Gary Hawkins, served beautifully. Covering the space in the backcourt, she made one shot after another. A trickle of sweat ran down the side of her face. She'd never played better! Tennis no longer seemed like hard work; it didn't even seem like something she had to think about. All the work she'd done with Lisa and Coach Barker was finally paying off. Her timing and reflexes were perfect!

But suddenly something broke her concentration—a noise on the other side of the court. An angry groan erupted from Simmie as he let a point slip by!

Palmer blinked and looked across the net. Simmie's green eyes were flashing angrily, and his face was red with exertion—and frustration. She remembered what he had said to her earlier: "Whenever I lose, I really hate the person . . ."

Palmer kept playing as well as she could, but inside she began to feel shaky. She had to work to keep her eye on the ball and she could actually feel Simmie glaring right at her.

Despite the look in Simmie's eye and the commotion in Palmer's mind, the two couples were still playing about even. If Palmer slipped up ever so slightly, Gary Hawkins' excellent timing made up the difference. On the other side of the net, Simmie's partner Megan was playing well, too. The audience seemed mesmerized as the ball went back and forth over and over again.

"This could go on forever," Rob whispered to Lisa.

"I know," Lisa replied tensely. "They're all so good!"

The two teams traded games until the score was 6–6. Then it was time for the "sudden death" tie-breaker. The first team to score five points would win.

Again, the players seemed perfectly matched, and soon it was 4-all! But then, playing for the final point, Megan suddenly made a weak shot. The ball sailed straight toward Palmer. It was the chance that she and Gary needed to win the tournament.

For a fraction of a second Palmer's eyes left the ball and met Simmie's angry gaze. And suddenly she knew—if she made the winning point, it would be the end of everything! He would never speak to her again, let alone take her to the Ardsley dance or be her pen pal. Her eyes came back to the tennis ball floating toward her. The moment seemed like an eternity. It was an easy shot. She knew she could make it.

With her racket held back, Palmer ran to meet the ball. The whole point of learning to play a game was playing your best. That's what Coach Barker had taught her. That's what her mind told her, too. But now her heart was saying something different. It wasn't the game that she wanted to win—it was Simmie! How could she enjoy winning the tournament if it meant losing him?

To the audience, what happened next looked like an unfortunate mistake: Palmer's racket just missed the ball by a hair.

"Oh, no!" Lisa groaned. "She missed it!"

"Too bad," Amy said disappointedly. "And she was playing so well, too."

The tournament was over. "Game, set, match to Simmie Randolph the Third, and Megan Morgan," Coach Barker announced. "The score is seven to six."

Palmer's head buzzed as she went through the motions of shaking her partner's hand; then she and Gary approached the net to shake hands with the winners. First Palmer shook hands with Megan. "Congratulations," she mumbled, pasting on a false smile.

"Congratulations yourself," Megan said generously. "You played a terrific game. There's nothing tougher than losing."

"Thanks," said Palmer, letting Megan's words sink in. Even though she'd thrown the game for a good cause, she felt empty inside. Maybe there *was* something tougher than losing—losing on purpose!

But when Simmie walked over to shake her hand, Palmer's face brightened. He didn't look the least bit angry anymore.

"You are a formidable opponent," he said with a grin.

"Thanks," Palmer said, "and congratulations." Her heart pounded as he looked into her face. His eyes had a mysterious twinkle in them.

"That last shot you tried to make was freaky," he said with a wink. "For a minute, I thought you were going to beat us."

"It was the spin on the ball," Palmer lied carefully. "Just bad luck I guess."

"Bad luck, huh?" Simmie echoed softly. As the two couples began walking off the court, he dropped back and whispered in Palmer's ear: "That was no bad luck."

Palmer stared straight ahead at Coach Barker and the Ardsley coach, who were waiting at the sideline. "What are you talking about?" she whispered back uncomfortably.

Simmie grinned and winked again. "You know what I mean," he gloated, stepping forward to take his prize. "I psyched you out!"

CHAPTER EIGHT

Monday morning, Miss Grayson stood at the door handing back the graded French homework.

"Well done, Palmer," she said. "I can tell you've been industrious."

Palmer smiled and said thank you. This wasn't the first time Miss Grayson had singled her out, but all the other times it had been for her slovenly work habits, not her industriousness.

"You're doing so well in every subject," Lisa marveled once she, Palmer, and Shanon were out the door.

"I want to stay on the tennis team," Palmer explained. Actually, she was surprised herself at how much her grades had come up. Being a good student had never been part of her self-image.

The three girls headed over to Booth to meet Amy. Then they planned to get some fruit from the dining hall and have a picnic. The rainy spell seemed over for good and the quad was bordered with a profusion of colorful flowers.

"I thought you'd be leaving the tennis team as soon as the round robin was over," Lisa said, giving Palmer a curious glance.

"I was planning to," Palmer confessed, "but I've decided that being on the team is more important."

"More important than Simmie?" Lisa razzed her.

"Nothing is more important than Simmie," Palmer blurted out in confusion. "What I meant is that playing on the team turned out to be more enjoyable than I thought it would be."

Lisa looked carefully at Palmer. It was hard to believe that this was the same Palmer who'd caused so much trouble in the suite all winter. The Palmer the Foxes knew was lazy and downright underhanded. She was someone who always put herself first. But this Palmer was different. She was making efforts in a lot of areas, including getting along with people.

On the way to Booth, the girls bumped into Dolores. The editor-in-chief of *The Ledger* and all-around super achiever was wearing a silk dress and pearls. With her long red hair done up in a bun, she almost looked old enough to be a teacher.

"I suppose you're wondering why I'm dressed this way," Dolores said with an air of self-importance. "I just had a conference with Miss Pryn. I've been named student representative to the faculty." She gave them a superior look. "I've got so much to do already. But I'm not one to shirk my responsibilities."

"You're certainly not," Lisa said flatly. Lisa thought that Dolores was a power hog.

73

"There are a lot of people breaking rules around here," Dolores added. "Miss Pryn wants a crackdown, and I agree with her."

Shanon squirmed. "Maybe some of the rules are too strict," she said faintly, "like the one about pets."

"Not at all," Dolores disagreed. "We're running a boarding school around here, not a menagerie. By the way," she added, "I'm glad I ran into you. I'd like you to do a story for the next *Ledger*."

"Fire away!" Shanon said eagerly.

"I want you to do a profile on a girl in your suite— Palmer Durand."

Palmer's cheeks reddened. Dolores was talking as if she wasn't there. "A story on me?" she cut in.

"You're a rising tennis star!" Dolores exclaimed, turning to gaze at her. "You're following in your mother's footsteps. I think that's interesting. Of course, I'm following in my mom's footsteps, too. She did everything but everything when she was at Alma."

"Sounds like a great story," Shanon said. "I'd love to do it!"

"Great!" Dolores said before hurrying off. "I always knew you'd be a fine addition to the *Ledger* staff."

"She is too weird for words," Palmer said, rolling her eyes behind Dolores's retreating back. "When you tried to get on *The Ledger* at the beginning of the school year, all she wanted you for was a gofer. Kate was the one who finally helped you get a story."

"Dolores does seem to like taking credit for things," Lisa observed.

"But she has a lot on the ball," Shanon objected. "I think her idea for a story on Palmer is super."

"No it isn't!" Palmer said suddenly. Lisa and Shanon looked at her. "I don't think you should do it."

"Why not?" Shanon asked. "I thought you'd like it. There will probably be a picture of you."

"I . . . I don't know," Palmer said. The thought of having a whole article written about her was incredible; especially if there was a picture. But a little voice inside said she didn't deserve it. After all, she had thrown the round robin.

"I hope you're not being hard on yourself for coming in second in the round robin," Shanon said.

"Your playing was fantastic," Lisa piped up, "even if you didn't win the last match. Both you and Simmie were incredible."

"I know," Palmer said. "If only . . ."

"If only what?" Shanon asked.

"If only I hadn't been . . . paired against him at the end," she replied, lowering her eyes. What would they think of her if they knew she had lost on purpose? She hoped that they would understand. After all, she'd had a good reason. If Palmer had won the match, Simmie would have hated her. "Come on," she said, changing the subject. "Let's find Amy."

The girls continued into Booth Hall and spotted Amy at the mailboxes.

"Anything from John?" Lisa asked.

"Nothing," Amy replied. "But I did get a letter from my friend Evon in Australia!"

Attacking her own box, Lisa came up empty. "I can't believe Rob hasn't written yet!" Tears of anger sparkled in her eyes. "He held my hand twice at the tennis match, but he didn't say anything about the dance at Ardsley. And now he's not even writing to me."

"Mars hasn't written, either," Shanon reported with concern. "And he didn't say more than three words to me the day of the round robin. On the other dates we had, he was so cheerful and talkative."

"Don't worry," Palmer said brightly. "I didn't get a letter from Simmie, either. That proves there's something wrong with the mail."

"Maybe Simmie didn't write to you," Lisa suggested.

"That's impossible," Palmer said. "He has to write to me to send my invitation to the dance. When he was at the round robin, he said he was going to."

"At least one of us has been invited," Amy said.

"Well, he didn't actually invite me," Palmer explained, "but he did say he wanted to talk to me about the dance."

"Is that the same as an invitation?" Shanon asked doubtfully.

"Of course it is," Palmer declared.

Hurrying through the lunch line in the dining hall, the Foxes grabbed some juice and apples. "That's not enough to stick to your ribs," Mrs. Butter scolded. The day's hot entree choices were roast beef with Yorkshire pudding or chipped beef on toast.

"We'd like to be able to *see* our ribs," Lisa sang out, stuffing a pear in her pocket. Thanks to Mrs. Butter's good cooking, Lisa had put on five extra pounds since September. No one would have ever called her overweight, but if her waist got any bigger, she'd never be able to zip up the antique gold dress she'd gotten from her grandmother. She planned to wear that gorgeous dress to the dance at Ardsley . . . *if* Rob invited her!

"Let's head for the river," Amy said, trotting off in front of the group. The hill behind the gym was carpeted with apple blossoms. "Since none of us got letters from The Unknown, I'll read you my letter from Evon," she offered.

"Evon sounds neat," Lisa said, finding a spot on the ground.

"She is," Amy replied. "And I've known her ever since nursery school. That's when we were living in Sydney." The daughter of a Chinese–American businessman, Amy had lived all over the world—including Australia, England, and Thailand.

Amy eagerly scanned her friend's letter while Shanon and Lisa bit into their fruit. Palmer stared down the hill with a dreamy expression. To think that only a while ago the river had been covered with ice, she mused. Now spring had changed everything. The next time Simmie came to Alma they'd go walking hand in hand by the river. She'd be wearing a beautiful dress, maybe the new yellow one. Then, for the dance at Ardsley, she'd wear her off-the-shoulder white satin. After all, it was probably semi-formal. . . .

Palmer's thoughts were interrupted by the sound of Lisa crunching into her apple. She looked up as Amy exclaimed, "This letter from Evon is great! Just listen!"

Dear Amy,

My father is coming to the states for a convention, and I am coming along! Are you able to see me one weekend? Pop will be travelling on to Boston, so if possible I would like to sleep one night at your school and take a train the following day to meet him. I don't think he'll have time to make the detour to Alma. So that is my solution. In any case, I am bound for your territory and I'm sure somehow we'll see one another. At least we'll be in the same hemisphere! Looking forward to your answer. This comes with much love.

> *Cheerio,*
> *Evon*

"Wow!" Lisa exclaimed. "Will you get to see her?"

"I'm sure going to try!" Amy said. "Evon and I used to have so much fun together. When we were four, we made up our own language."

"Like what?" Shanon asked.

"Appla-pappla!" Amy exlaimed, laughing. "Whenever we agreed on something, we said that."

"Sounds cute," Palmer said.

"That was nothing!" Amy continued. "We used to have this game where we would read each other's minds."

"Come on!" Lisa said. "That's impossible."

"It's not," Amy insisted. "I'll show you." She gave Lisa a teasing look. "L. M. L. R. W.," she said. "What am I thinking?"

Lisa rolled her eyes. "Lisa McGreevy likes Rob Williams," she guessed, giggling.

Shanon laughed. "That wasn't very hard to guess. That's all Lisa *ever* thinks about!"

"Let's try a more difficult one," Amy suggested. "Palmer, look into my eyes and concentrate. P. D. I. A. G. T. P. What am I thinking?"

Palmer gasped. "Palmer Durand is a great tennis player!"

"Correct," Amy said, smiling.

"Let me try now," Lisa said. She held up a pear and an apple core. "I. S. H."

Amy chortled. "That's easy, too. 'I'm still hungry!' "

"Lisa's always hungry," Palmer giggled.

"If Evon is anything like she was when you were little," Shanon said, "the two of you are going to have loads of fun together."

"I hope so," Amy said. "Maybe I ought to tone myself down a bit, though. Evon has a good sense of humor, but she's kind of quiet and shy. Her parents are really conservative. They always used to dress her up in little pink outfits for their tea parties. She probably still dresses that way."

"What does she look like?" Lisa asked. "I mean her hair and stuff?"

"She has thick red hair and she's very short," Amy reported. "I was always much taller."

"And when was the last time you saw her?" Palmer asked.

Amy counted on her fingers. "Six whole years ago. When I was seven."

"That's a lifetime!" Shanon exclaimed. "I hope Miss

79

Grayson will give you permission to have a guest."

"Maybe Evon can sleep in the sitting room," Lisa suggested.

"No, let her sleep in our room!" Palmer said.

"Thanks." Amy smiled. "That's a better idea. I'll sleep on the floor and let Evon have my bed."

Lisa chuckled. "That's nice of you."

"Well, she was always very proper," Amy explained.

Shanon was the only one not smiling. "At least two of us have something to look forward to," she said, playing with a blade of grass. "Amy has a friend coming, and Palmer is going to the Ardsley dance."

"I want to go to the dance, too!" Lisa groaned.

"Then go for it!" Palmer said brightly. "I wanted to play in the round robin with Simmie and be invited to the dance more than anything in the world, and I made it happen."

"You did achieve your goal," Lisa admitted. "But when it comes to Rob Williams, I don't know what more I can do about it."

"There is something else you could do," Shanon said thoughtfully. "And I could do the same with Mars."

"What's that?" Lisa asked.

Shanon laughed. "B. H.—read my mind!"

Amy chuckled. "Be honest?"

"Correct!" Shanon said, surprised. "That was a hard one."

"I *have* been honest," Lisa said stubbornly.

"Not entirely," Shanon told her. "You haven't admitted to Rob that you were really mad at him. And you haven't told him you want to be invited to the dance."

"Right," Palmer agreed.

"You think I should invite myself?" Lisa exclaimed.

"Why not?" Palmer said. "We've invited the Unknowns to lots of things here at Alma. It's only fair that they should invite us back."

"Ummm," said Lisa, "I see your point."

"And I have to be more honest with Mars," Shanon declared, "so that he can be more honest with me. I want to see him again as soon as possible."

"How come?" Amy teased. "Because you like his mirrored glasses?"

"No, because I like him," Shanon replied. "I didn't know how much until I got worried about him. I really want to go to the dance with him."

"What do we have to lose?" Lisa asked. "We'll just come out and say what's on our minds. We'll try Palmer's way."

"Yes, honesty is the best policy," Shanon agreed.

"I hope it works out," Palmer said, tossing down her apple core. Lisa whipped a camera out of her bookbag and took a picture of it.

"I thought you were taking pictures of found objects."

"I've branched out," Lisa explained. "Now I'm taking pictures of any object that interests me."

"What's so interesting about an apple core?" Shanon said, laughing.

Lisa snapped another picture and put down her camera. "This, my dear Foxes, is not just an ordinary core. It is the apple core of the famous Palmer Durand, romantic advisor and tennis star!"

81

Palmer laughed, too. "The next thing I know you'll be taking pictures of my tennis shoes."

"Why not?" said Lisa, snapping a picture of Palmer's foot.

Amy and Shanon giggled and tossed up some apple blossoms. Palmer sighed contentedly as the petals fell over her. Being important felt great.

CHAPTER NINE

Interview for the Alma Stephens Ledger by Shanon Davis

I met Palmer Durand in the library coffee shop for our interview. Although we live in the same suite, we decided that a more formal setting would be appropriate. An interviewer's job is to paint a true portrait of an individual. I will let Palmer's own candid remarks speak for her.

SD: What was it like growing up in Florida?

PD: What do you mean?

SD: Perhaps that's too vague a question. Your childhood must have been wonderful.

PD: I can't remember it much.

SD: Your mother was known as a brilliant athlete in her days at Alma. She must be proud to see you following in her footsteps.

PD: I'm not sure she knows about it yet. But I hope she'll be proud when she does hear.

SD: Did she teach you to play tennis?

PD: No, she never played with me. I had the best instructors, though.

SD: But I'm sure your parents encouraged you.

PD: My dad doesn't live with us. He lives in California.

SD: So your mom pushed you to excel?

PD: I'm not sure what you mean by that. She did send me to tennis camp. She's not much of a pusher.

SD: Let's talk about your likes and dislikes. What comes to mind?

PD: I don't understand.

SD: Our readers will be interested in the truth about you.

PD: The truth?

SD: Your true feelings about things. What do you enjoy most in the world?

PD: Dressing up. No, scratch that—I never thought I'd say there was something I enjoy more. But lately, I like sweating.

SD: Can you explain what you mean by that?

PD: I never was a sweater. I hated tennis camp. I would rather have sat by the pool all summer, but my mother had set it up so I had to be active. Now that I'm on the tennis team, I've changed. The more I sweat, the better I feel.

SD: The activity makes you feel good?

PD: Yes. That's thanks to Coach Barker.

SD: Would you say that the coach is your inspiration then?

PD: She wasn't in the beginning, but she is now. I

never thought I wanted to be like anybody, but maybe I'd like to be like her.

SD: A tennis coach?

PD: Oh, no. Just the way she is.

SD: How's that?

PD: Coach Barker doesn't pull any punches. I'd like to be like that someday. The same as she is . . . as a person.

SD: Even though you didn't come in on the winning team during the round robin, being selected to compete in the final match was a great honor. You must be happy.

PD: Happy? I suppose so. Yes, I'm very happy.

Palmer ran all the way to the courts. Running was something she'd never liked doing. She had told the truth to Shanon in her interview. Sweating was no longer a problem.

Regular practice didn't start for another hour, and Palmer wanted to find Megan Morgan to warm up with. Megan was good. Of course, Palmer would never know just how good. She would always wonder whether she and Gary could have won the match against Megan and Simmie. Deep in her heart she regretted not giving herself the chance to make the winning point. But it was worth it not to have lost Simmie.

Rounding the corner beyond the quad, Palmer caught sight of Megan. The older girl was already playing with someone. Palmer was startled to see that it was a boy. Coach Barker was seated near the sideline watching. As

Palmer came closer and recognized Megan's partner, she stopped short. Megan was playing with Gary Hawkins—Palmer's own partner in the final match of the round robin. She turned on her heel to walk in the other direction, just as Megan and Gary came off the court.

"Hey, Palmer!" Megan yelled.

Palmer stopped and turned back as Megan and Gary started walking toward her.

"Remember Gary Hawkins from Ardsley?" Megan asked.

"Sure," Palmer said. "Hi, Gary."

"Nice to see you again," the boy said graciously.

"Gary and I are competing in a mixed-doubles competition downstate," Megan explained excitedly. "The coach gave us permission to practice together."

"Great," Palmer said, feeling uncomfortable.

Coach Barker came over to join them. "It's a good competition," she said, smiling at Palmer. "Maybe something you can shoot for someday, Durand."

Palmer gulped. "Love to."

"I'm sure you'll have no problem," Gary said, smiling. "You're an excellent player."

"No, I'm not," Palmer found herself saying. "I mean . . . we lost because of me."

"We were both out there," Gary objected. "How come it's your fault?"

Palmer looked down. "No reason. I'm only sorry that we didn't win."

"Better luck next time," Gary said lightly. "Anyway, it was just an exhibition. It wasn't important."

"The important thing is to play your best," Coach Barker added, "and not get hung up on winning. The biggest opponent you've got out there is yourself." She turned her sharp gaze on Palmer. "You agree, Durand?"

"Sure," Palmer said, turning away to avoid the coach's eyes.

"Where are you going?" Megan called. "Gary and I are finished. How about a warm-up?"

"I have some things to do before practice," Palmer called over her shoulder. Seeing Gary had taken the fun out of the day. No matter how unimportant the round robin had been to him, Palmer knew she had been dishonest. And there was something else she knew as well . . . that no matter what she'd told Shanon in the interview, no matter how much she wanted to, she could never be like Coach Barker.

CHAPTER TEN

Dear Mars,

I would like to be perfectly honest with you. I wish you would tell me more about your problem. That is what friends are for. And I hope you think of me as a friend, not just a pen pal. I have told you a lot about myself since we have been writing. But you haven't done the same. I am a very trustworthy person if that's what you're worried about. My sister Doreen has told me lots of secrets, and I never told anyone. And I told her some, too. Once in my old school some mean girls made fun of me because of something personal about my looks. They really hurt my feelings and made me not want to go to school. I felt dumb telling my parents about it. But I told Doreen and talking to her made me feel better. She even gave me some advice that worked about not letting those girls make fun of me anymore. I know your problem is different, but it still might help to share it.

If you are really a pen pal, *then write and tell me what's on your mind.*

Yours truly,
Shanon

Dear Shanon,
    Your letter was nice. Thank you. I didn't mean to hurt your feelings by not letting you in on what's been eating me. I really do like you. You are not just a pen pal to me. Otherwise, I wouldn't have kept writing all these months. I am not the type of person who gets into writing to people I don't know just for the heck of it. I kept you for a pen pal because I wanted to get to know you. Now I see that you don't know me very well. How can you if I don't tell you anything that's really going on with me? I don't see how you can help, but this is the problem—my dad has lost his job. When I went home for the break, my mom was upset. My dad was down in a way I have not seen before. I think I should get a job myself.

Sincerely,
Mars

Dear Mars,
    The fact that your father has lost his job is upsetting, I can imagine. My dad owns a garage in Brighton and once there was a fire and he lost a lot. Part of our house was burned too. It took a lot for Dad to build the business back up again. My mom had never worked before, and she had to get a job as a secretary. We did not have much money for a while. Maybe you could get a part-time job at school

to help out. What happened to your pen-holder business?
Maybe there is something else you can invent. I would help
you sell whatever it is at Alma. Whatever happens, please
remember that I am your friend.

Fondly,
Shanon

Dear Shanon,
   You have started my brain buzzing. I have a new idea for
a bunch of buttons with slogans. I also called my dad and
talked to him. I wanted to find out what the real story
was—that is, whether my family is out-and-out broke. My
dad says we are okay, but I would still feel better making
some money on my own. I'm putting my feelers out for the
summer. I plan to go to summer session, so if you know of
anything in the area, please let me know. Thanks for
listening.

Yours truly,
Mars

P.S. There is a dance coming up at Ardsley, semi-formal.
Enclosed is an invitation.
P.P.S. Here are some possible button slogans:
   DON'T BOTHER ME! I'M BREATHING!
   DON'T SAY I'M HANDSOME, JUST KISS ME
   NAPOLEON WAS SHORT
   BE KIND TO LICE
   PREPPIES, THE NEW ENDANGERED SPECIES

Dear Mars,
   Thank you for inviting me to the dance. I would love to

come. *The button slogans are funny! How about, I'D RATHER BE EATING CHOCOLATE! or READ MY MIND! Also, if you are going to be in the area for part of the summer, my father might need somebody at the garage. I will ask him.*

Sincerely,
Shanon

Dear Rob,
   I want to be perfectly honest with you. And I hope you will be honest with me. I was still mad at you when we were at the round robin. Now it seems like a stupid reason. I thought since I live in Pennsylvania that you should work there this summer on the dairy farm. I thought that this would be proof that you are more than just a pen pal and are my special friend. I definitely think of you as a special friend. But I suppose if somebody offered me a chance to go learn how to paint in Paris or something I would not turn it down just to be working in the same state with you. So I finally understand why you decided to take the job in Alaska.
   Things are going along pretty well for me these days. Some of my photographs are going to be hanging in Booth Hall at an exhibition. There is one of an apple core that people seem to like especially. I don't know whether things look different through the lens of a camera or if people just don't really stop to look at things with their bare eyeballs. Whatever the reason, everyday objects look a lot more interesting in a picture because you have to stop and look. Perhaps the next time you visit Alma my pictures will still

be hanging. We don't have any more social events coming up for a while. Do you have any social events coming up at Ardsley?

Yours truly,
Lisa

Dear Lisa,

Sorry. I didn't realize I was insulting you or the state of Pennsylvania by deciding I didn't want to work there this summer. I had a good time at the round robin myself. I didn't even know you were mad at me. But thanks for telling me so that I have a chance to apologize. I admire your frankness and maturity. Musk ox are a rare species and that is one reason why I think my choice to go to Alaska is important. But I hope that you will still write to me this summer from Pennsylvania. I'll need your letters more than ever.

Yours truly,
Rob

P.S. To answer your question, there is a dance coming up at Ardsley.

Dear Rob,

By mentioning the dance at Ardsley, did you mean to invite me? I would like to know for sure. If you are inviting me, I would like to go.

Yours,
Lisa

Dear Lisa,

Enclosed is an invitation to the dance on the 18th. Consider yourself invited. I think the reason why I didn't send it before is because when I mentioned the dance in an earlier letter you didn't say anything about it. I thought you might be going with someone else. I'm sure you are very popular.

Rob

Dear Rob,

Thanks for the invitation. I look forward to seeing you. I have read up on musk ox. It is neat of you to think about working with a species that needs protection. Even if somebody else had asked me to the dance, I would have wanted to go with you.

Lisa

Dear Evon,

All I have to say about your impending visit is: aggro, so excellent, rad, super cool! Appla-pappla! It is the most exciting thing. It will make my year. Tell your pa yes that you can stay with me. I cannot wait to introduce you to the Foxes and show you my school. I love it here. Spring is incredible. Don't forget to pack some lightweight clothes. Hurry up from the land down under!

Your friend always,
Amy

Dear Simmie,

Playing with you in the round robin was a very special experience. I am only sorry that we were not paired up at the end for the final match. I have been waiting for a letter from you. At the round robin you mentioned the dance at your school. Did you send the invitation yet? I didn't get it. I hope it was not lost in the mail.

Yours truly,
Palmer

CHAPTER ELEVEN

"Tell me which earrings look best," Lisa said, "the gold hoops or the dangly rhinestone ones."

"I like the rhinestones," Shanon answered.

"Yes," agreed Brenda Smith. "The rhinestones are much more semi-formal looking."

"But my dress is gold," Lisa argued, holding one of each next to her face. "It's really a problem."

Amy looked up from her math homework in annoyance. Since Lisa and Shanon had received invitations to the Ardsley dance, the suite had been as crazy as the back stage of a rock concert! Every day Lisa invited some new person over to check out her clothes and chatter all night. Amy wished she could share their excitement, but she wasn't going to the dance. She and John were still having a cold war. They hadn't talked about the disagreement over his poem at the round robin, and they hadn't written to one another since.

"Are we disturbing you?" Shanon asked, trying to be

considerate. Shanon had a limited wardrobe, so finding something to wear to the dance had become a major concern for her also. The loveseat was piled high with dresses from both Lisa's and Brenda's closets that she was considering.

"What makes you think you're disturbing me?" Amy quipped, sarcastically. "I always do my homework in a dressing room."

Lisa ruffled Amy's hair. "Don't be such a grouch. If you want to go to the dance, you can ask John to invite you, just like I asked Rob to invite me."

"He has to write to me first," Amy said stubbornly.

"I hear you have a friend coming from Australia," Brenda said, handing a green spangled dress to Shanon.

Amy nodded. "Evon. She's too neat for words. Too bad she's not coming the night of the dance!"

Kate knocked on the door and opened it without waiting for an answer. "Anybody who's been invited to the Ardsley dance, fill out one of these to get your passes." She thrust some papers in Shanon's direction.

"Too much!" Lisa exclaimed. "What is Miss Pryn afraid of? A jailbreak?"

"We have to know who's going where and when," Kate said officiously. She wiped her glasses off on the tail of her sweater.

"Are you going?" Lisa asked, watching her closely.

Kate smiled shyly. "As a matter of fact, I have two invitations."

"Two invitations!" Lisa gasped in disbelief. In Lisa's opinion, nobody at Alma was as dweeby as Kate. It was enough of a mystery what Lisa's brother Reggie saw in her. Had she actually gotten another boy interested, too?

"How did you manage that?" Brenda asked in awe.

"Who are the two guys who asked you?" Shanon chimed in.

"I only got one invitation from a boy," Kate admitted. "Reggie McGreevy. But I've also been invited as a member of the Alma Social Committee."

Lisa's eyes narrowed. Reggie was inviting Kate and hadn't told her about it. That hurt her feelings. When they'd lived at home together, they'd told each other everything. "What are you going to wear?" Lisa quipped. "A wool skirt?"

"I've got a nice dress," Kate said happily. "I have to look good, since I'm also representing the committee. I'm supposed to check out the Ardsley D.J. in case we want him for our dances."

"I thought Dolores always did that," Shanon said.

Kate drew closer. "Dolores is going to Princeton that weekend," she gossiped.

"Princeton!" Brenda's mouth dropped open. "Grown men go there!"

"Speaking of grownups—has anyone heard the latest about Miss Grayson?" Lisa spoke up, joining the huddle. "She's going to the Ardsley dance as an escort—with Mr. Seganish!"

"That can't be true!" Shanon wailed. "Poor Mr. Griffith!"

"Maybe they had a fight over a poem or something, like Amy and John," Lisa speculated.

Amy cleared her throat loudly. "What is this? A hen party? You'd think that the most important thing in the world was the Ardsley dance!" She glanced at the party dresses defiantly. "I'm glad I'm not going. And if I was going, I wouldn't wear all that lace stuff!"

"What would you wear?" Lisa challenged.

"My motorcycle jacket!" Amy exclaimed. "With nothing but a Danskin underneath! Maybe I'll crash the party!"

The door to the suite opened and Palmer slunk in. Her face was pale, and she looked as if she'd been crying. "Something awful's happened," she announced. She was holding her tennis racket in one hand and a piece of paper in the other.

"What's wrong?" Shanon cried.

"Sit down," Amy said.

"You look sick," Brenda volunteered.

"How awful is it?" Lisa asked.

"Very awful," Palmer answered dramatically. A tear rolled down her face as she took a seat.

Lisa gave Brenda and Kate an intense look. "If you don't mind, I think she needs some privacy."

Brenda grabbed her clothes and scooted, while Kate nodded understandingly and backed out the door.

"Thanks," Palmer said with a sniffle. "I don't exactly want the whole world to know about this."

"But you can tell us," Shanon said, gently.

"You can tell us anything," Amy added.

Palmer handed the piece of paper she was holding to Lisa. "See for yourself."

Dear Palmer,

I did not send you an invitation to the dance because I don't have another one. I have sent out the one I have to my girlfriend. I guess you don't know her. She goes to Brier Hall.

Yours truly,
Simmie Randolph III

"Oh, no!" Lisa groaned.

"That crumb!" Amy declared angrily.

"How could he do that to you?" Shanon gasped.

Feeling their empathy, Palmer broke down. "I don't know. I really . . . liked him," she sobbed. "I thought *I* was his girlfriend. And all the time . . . he had . . . another one!"

"And she goes to Brier Hall!" Amy sputtered. "This is treason!"

"Betrayal!" Lisa said, pacing. "The Foxes of the Third Dimension and The Unknown made a bargain. We agreed to write to each other. We agreed that when there were dances—"

"The Unknown never agreed to that," Shanon interrupted.

"They didn't out-and-out agree," Lisa sputtered, "but they should have known! Simmie Randolph should have known that if he was Palmer's pen pal, he was supposed to invite her to the dance!"

"I agree!" Amy said. "And if he was going to invite someone else, it certainly shouldn't have been some Brier girl! Brier Hall is our rival!"

Shanon offered a tissue, and Palmer took it and blew her nose. "Thanks for being on my side," she said. "After this, the only conclusion I can draw is that Simmie Randolph is a creep."

"A first-class creep," Lisa added. She picked up the letter and made a gesture to rip it. "May I?"

"Let me," Palmer said, snatching the letter away. She ripped it in half, balled it into two little pieces, then threw them into the wastebasket. "If it's the last thing I do, I'm going to find a way to get back at him," she declared vengefully.

"We'll help you," Amy volunteered. "Nobody chills my roommate and gets away with it."

"I think the best thing to do is forget about him," Shanon ventured.

"How can I forget!" Palmer exclaimed. Fresh tears sprang to her eyes. "I sacrificed a lot for him! If it hadn't been for him, I would have won the round robin!"

There was a pause, and then Lisa spoke up. "Well, Simmie may be a creep, but he had no control over your not being his partner."

"That's not what I mean," Palmer blurted out. "I could have won! If it hadn't been for his psyching me out like he did! He told me that whoever he lost to, he hated! I didn't want him to hate me, so I—"

"Hold on," Amy said. "Are you telling us what I think you are?"

"You lost the match on purpose?" Shanon asked, horrified.

Palmer paled. "I . . . I played my best up until the end,"

she confessed with a swallow. "But at the very last minute when I saw Simmie across the net I—"

"You threw the match," Lisa said flatly. Her dark eyes were accusing. "And just the other day you were lecturing us all about being honest. You almost had me convinced you were really changing."

"Wait—" Palmer said weakly. "It wasn't my fault. Simmie psyched me out."

"And you gave in," Lisa said. "You cheated!"

"It was only an exhibition match!" Palmer argued. "Nobody really cared."

"We cared," Shanon said, her bottom lip quivering. "You played so well. We thought you were going to win. We—"

"What's this *we* stuff?" Palmer exploded. "Anybody would think I was trying to win the tournament for your sakes! I was playing for myself, so how I played was my decision!"

"I guess I see your point," Shanon said, trying to be understanding. "I didn't mean—"

"Well, I don't see Palmer's point at all!" Lisa broke in angrily. "And I'm not going to listen to any more of what she has to say! I'm going to my room and open the window."

"I have some studying to do myself," Shanon said, following behind her. On her way out of the sitting room, she glanced at Palmer sadly. "I guess we shouldn't be upset about this," she apologized. "It was probably hard for you to do something . . . like that. . . ."

Palmer looked away in frustration. "It was just a stupid

game," she muttered. Amy was the only one left for her to talk to. "I guess you're mad at me, too?"

Amy shrugged. "Not exactly," she said. "I guess I just don't get it. I can't imagine doing something like that for any boy."

"Thanks a lot," Palmer said bitterly. "If I hadn't told you all what I'd done, you wouldn't be able to give me all this grief. The next time somebody says I can tell them anything, remind me not to believe them!"

"You asked me a question," Amy countered. "I'm just being honest."

"I don't need you to be honest," Palmer cried, "I need you to be my friend! But I can see you're not, so forget it!" And tossing her racket onto the loveseat, she slammed out of the door.

Lisa paced the floor with her flashlight. It was more than half an hour after lights-out, and Palmer still wasn't back.

"We have to report this to Miss Grayson," Shanon said, wringing the hem of her nightgown. "Suppose Palmer did something silly like run away."

"She wouldn't leave her clothes," Amy said.

"We *were* pretty hard on her," Lisa argued. "Maybe she was too ashamed to face us."

"Maybe she was scared that we would tell somebody else what she did," Shanon reasoned.

Amy shook her head in disagreement. "I'm sure Palmer didn't run away. She even left her pocketbook and her

102

charge cards. She's probably hiding out in somebody else's room."

"Hiding from us," Shanon said softly. "We shouldn't have been so mean to her."

"But throwing the match was so underhanded," Lisa argued, "especially after I'd helped her. And we all wanted her to win!"

"She wanted to win, too," Amy said sadly. "The person she hurt most was herself."

"And her partner," Lisa pointed out. "Too bad Simmie Randolph gets off scot-free."

"This is mostly Simmie's fault," Amy agreed. "First he sends all those mushy letters to Palmer, then he psyches her out on the tennis court on purpose, and then he dumps her."

Lisa crossed to the desk with her flashlight. "I'm so mad I have to eat." She rummaged in a drawer for some candy bars.

"I don't think we should be too mad at Palmer," Shanon said.

"It's Simmie Randolph I'm mad at now," Lisa declared, ripping into the chocolate.

"There's got to be a way of getting back at him," Amy began. "If Palmer showed up at the dance with someone else . . . then Simmie would be burned."

"He'd see he's not the only boy in the world!" Shanon added.

"All we have to do is get Palmer another date," Lisa said. "But who?"

Amy squinted across the room at the clock on the bookshelf. "It's already after ten-thirty. Even if Palmer is hiding in another girl's room, I think we ought to tell somebody," she said.

"Let's tell Kate," Shanon said, jumping up. "Maybe she'll give us permission to look for Palmer."

"And if we don't find her in Fox Hall," Lisa added, "we'll tell Miss Grayson."

The girls padded down the hall and knocked softly on Kate's door. Kate opened right away. She was wearing a flannel bathrobe.

"Come in!" she whispered, motioning them inside. And there, huddled on the foot of Kate's bed eating gumdrops, was Palmer.

"There you are!" Lisa hissed. "We were worried about you."

"I thought you didn't like me anymore," Palmer said quietly.

Kate motioned Lisa, Shanon, and Amy to the corner. "I found her crying in the common room. She told me what happened. This Simmie Randolph sounds like bad news."

Lisa turned to Palmer. "Did you tell Kate the whole story?" she asked curiously.

Palmer nodded. "I feel for Palmer," Kate said. "I know what it's like to be dumped by a boy. It happened to me once."

"It does hurt to be dumped," Lisa commiserated. "It's never happened to me. But I wouldn't wish it on anybody."

"Except Simmie Randolph," Amy said, meaningfully.

She walked over to Palmer. "Sorry we were so hard on you."

"I'm the one who's sorry," Palmer said, sniffling mournfully. "I'm a disgrace to everyone."

"No you're not," Shanon protested. "Like you said, it was only an exhibition match. It was mainly for fun."

"What about Gary Hawkins?" Palmer pointed out. "He would have liked winning. And what about Coach Barker? She gave me a chance and encouraged me. What about my mother? I'd finally done something she was interested in. I let all of them down just to make Simmie happy."

"Simmie's a smooth operator," Lisa said, softening. "You're probably not the first girl who's done something dumb for him."

"And I won't be the last," Palmer said. "I can't believe he's got a girlfriend. I feel so stupid."

"You can learn from your mistake," Amy said generously. "Now all you have to do is teach Randolph a lesson!"

"But how?" Palmer said.

"We have an idea," Lisa explained. "You could go to the dance with another date and show Simmie up."

"All we need is a stray Ardie," Shanon said.

"That's impossible," Palmer said. "The whole reason we started pen pals was because we didn't know any Ardies. How are we going to come up with another one so quickly?"

"I may have the answer to your problem," Kate declared. "I told you I have two invitations."

"But how could Palmer come as a Social Committee rep?" Lisa asked.

"She can't," Kate replied. "But she *can* come as Reggie's date."

"Reggie McGreevy's date?" Palmer said faintly. Lisa's egghead brother wasn't exactly what she had envisioned as the boy to inspire Simmie's jealousy. "No thanks. I couldn't."

"It's your chance to get to the dance," Amy argued.

"And it's only a way of getting in the door," Kate warned. "All I'll ask Reggie to do is put your name down on the guest list. At the dance, he'll go back to being my date."

"It *would* be fun to go," Palmer said, perking up.

"You can meet other Ardsley boys that way!" Shanon said brightly.

"There's one other condition," Kate said, crossing to her desk chair. "If I do get Palmer into the dance, she has to do something for me."

"You name it," Palmer said.

"It's risky," Kate warned. "If you get caught . . ."

"What do you want her to do?" Shanon asked nervously.

Kate smiled. "It has to do with a certain friend of mine." She scooped up something from the floor beneath her desk. In the moonlight they could barely make out the small furry form—a sleeping Tickle.

CHAPTER TWELVE

Amy stood alone at the school gate. The entrance driveway to Alma was lined with tall poplars. She could hardly remember the day last fall when she'd driven in for the first time with her dad. Before Alma Stephens, Amy had lived with her family in so many places. Now, for most of the year, Alma was her home.

Her heart beat faster as a cab approached the gate. Taxis didn't often come to Alma. Perhaps it was Evon. Maybe her dad hadn't been able to drive her. Amy nervously smoothed down her normally spiked black hair. Remembering how conservative Evon's family was, Amy had worn a simple blue dress and hoped she looked normal.

The cab pulled up, and Amy took a few steps forward. Her heart sunk with disappointment when the girl inside got out. She had red hair like Evon, but the cut was very trendy and this girl was much too tall. Besides, she was wearing very far-out clothes—tight jeans and a shiny blue tuxedo jacket. As the girl pulled an instrument case and a knapsack out of the cab, Amy noticed she was wearing roller skates!

The girl paid the driver and smiled again at Amy. "G'day mate, I hope I'm in the right place. Alma Stephens?"

Amy's mouth dropped open at the sound of the unmistakable Australian accent. "Evon?" she called.

The girl's freckled face lit up with her grin. "Is that you, Amy?"

Amy ran, Evon skated, and they collided in a big bear hug.

"You look so different!" Amy exclaimed. "I didn't recognize you!"

"Yes, I've shot up, eh?" Evon said. "I'm five feet, eight inches."

"And the clothes?" Amy asked.

Evon shrugged. "I always dress this way. As for the skates, I didn't know how far your dorm would be from the gate. I wanted to come on my own from town, so I asked Dad not to drive me. I have to meet him in Boston tomorrow night."

"It's outrageous that you're here!" Amy exclaimed, grabbing the knapsack. "I see you brought your violin with you."

"Yes," Evon said, picking up the instrument case. "But this one's an electric. I've branched out from just classical."

"Outrageous," Amy said again. "Come on! Fox Hall is this way!" She started toward the dorm with Evon skating at her side.

"To tell the truth," Evon admitted, "I didn't know it

was you either when I drove up. From the way you wrote about your dad not liking the way you dress, I thought you'd look a bit more rebellious."

Amy laughed. "I usually do! But today I'm dressed for *your* benefit."

"You're kidding!" Evon said. "I must not come across very accurately in my letters."

"Well, I also thought your dad might be with you," Amy explained. "I remember how . . ."

"How stuffy he is?" Evon giggled. "He hasn't changed, though he's great in a lot of other ways. He let me come on this trip."

"You must be wiped out," said Amy. "It's twenty-three hours on the plane, isn't it?"

"My dad's suffering from jet lag, all right. *He's* tired."

"What about you?" Amy asked.

Evon shrugged. "I'm wired."

When they got to the suite, Lisa, Shanon, and Palmer were all waiting, curious to meet Amy's shy friend from Australia.

"I'm Evon Raven," she announced, skating right in and shaking hands with everyone. "Don't tell me who you are! Let me guess!"

The three Foxes gaped in amazement while Evon pointed them out. "You're Palmer—you've got blonde hair; and that's got to be Lisa—very gorgeous and dramatic; and the intelligent-looking one is Shanon. She's the writer."

The girls laughed. "I guess Amy pegged us in her letters," Shanon said.

Evon grinned. "They're detailed, all right."

"I have an idea!" Amy said. "I've got roller skates—"

"Great!" Evon said. "Let's go on a wheel hike!"

In no time, the two old friends were touring the campus. "Shall we stop in for one of Mrs. Butter's meals?" Evon said gaily.

"Wow!" Amy exclaimed. "You do remember everything I've written to you!"

"I enjoy your letters so much," Evon said. "Don't ever stop writing, okay?"

"I won't if you won't," Amy promised.

They took a rest on a bench outside of Booth Hall, then decided to go in for some ice-cream cones. After unlacing their skates, they walked in stockinged feet to the snack bar.

"Mind if I check my mail?" Amy asked on the way.

"Not at all," Evon said. "Still got that boy pen pal?"

"I'm not really sure," Amy answered. "We haven't been writing much." She pulled out a letter. It was from John.

"Your lucky day, eh?" Evon said, peering over her shoulder.

They sat down on the floor in the hall, and Amy opened the envelope.

Dear Amy,

> *Girls are the greatest*
> *Independent or not*
> *Boys need them in all ways*
> *Preppie, Scholar or Jock.*
> *So come all ye of the opposite sex*
> *Let's make amends*

110

Let's dance and sing—
And above all be friends!
Whether I am a chauvinist or not I don't know. My other
poem was lousy because it was so abstract. I wasn't
writing about a real girl playing ball or climbing moun-
tains. I was writing about my muse. I guess an up person
like you doesn't have problems with being inspired. Any-
way, PLEASE COME TO THE DANCE AT ARDSLEY!
                              Your ever-lovin' pen pal,
                              John

"Is that ever cute!" Evon said. "Give him a break."

"Okay," Amy laughed.

Evon winked. "Bet he's *cute,* too."

Amy smiled happily. "Very!"

"What a marvelous idea pen pals is," Evon exclaimed. "I think I might try the same thing in my school in Sydney."

"Good luck," Amy said. "It can get complicated."

Evon shrugged. "Probably only if you make it that way."

They walked down the hall to the snack bar. "You still like chocolate ice cream?" Amy asked.

"No, peppermint's my favorite now," Evon answered. "You still like strawberry?"

Amy shook her head. "My current favorite is chocolate marshmallow."

The girls got their cones and went back outdoors to eat them. Watching Evon, Amy was amazed at how much she'd changed.

"Good ice cream," Evon said agreeably.

"Appla-pappla!" Amy said with a giggle.

Evon looked at her, gray eyes misting with emotion.

"I . . . G . . . Y . . . M . . . F.," she said softly.

Amy got the message. "Thanks," she said. "I'm glad you're my friend, too!"

Some things never change.

CHAPTER THIRTEEN

"Is everything all set?" Kate whispered, coming into the suite. She was carrying a big box wrapped like a present.

"You look really nice," Shanon exclaimed.

Lisa stared in amazement. In her long-sleeved blue flowered dress and with her hair pulled back, Kate did look less dweeby than usual. In fact, Lisa had to admit, Kate looked pretty good.

"Palmer's about to make her entrance," Amy said, hurrying into the sitting room. She was wearing an exotic-looking green dress that her aunt in Taiwan had sent. Her thin arms were loaded with bracelets.

"Look at Amy!" Shanon gasped. "That's much better than wearing a leotard and your motorcycle jacket."

"I guess," Amy agreed, squirming in the close-fitting dress.

"You look gorgeous," Lisa assured her, then turned back to the mirror for a final check. When all was said and done, she'd decided against both the rhinestones and the gold hoops, choosing instead to wear feather earrings with her grandmother's antique gold dress. "It's okay to wear something old-fashioned looking as long as you have on something modern to clash with it," she explained confidently.

"My dress is so plain next to everybody else's," Shanon said. In the end she'd decided not to borrow but to wear the same pink dress she wore to everything.

Lisa tossed her a tube of lipstick. "You're fine. All you need is more color."

Kate looked at her watch. "What's keeping Palmer? The bus will be outside. We want to get on it before Miss Grayson."

"We should try to be the first ones on," Amy agreed, glancing uneasily at the box Kate had brought in with her. "If we all sit together in the back, it'll be safer."

"I'm ready to come out!" Palmer sang from the bedroom.

"Give her a lot of compliments," Amy said hurriedly just as Palmer emerged in her off-the-shoulder white satin dress. Her beautiful face was made up meticulously and every shiny blonde hair was in place. She was wearing dangly rhinestone earrings and high-heeled white shoes.

"How do I look?" she asked expectantly.

"Incredible!" Lisa said

"Like Princess Di," Shanon offered sincerely.

"I think you have on too much perfume," Kate said, sniffing.

"Maybe I shouldn't go," Palmer said suddenly. "What if I get there and Simmie doesn't even notice me?"

"He'll notice you!" Amy encouraged. "Everyone will!"

"And you have to come now," Kate insisted. "Otherwise, who's going to be responsible for . . ." She glanced at the gift-wrapped box on the floor.

"You can smuggle it over yourself," Palmer told Kate.

"A deal's a deal," Kate said, getting excited. "We both know that getting caught smuggling this box has far worse consequences for me than you. Besides, I've never broken a rule before. I just couldn't."

"Not even for Tickle?" Lisa exclaimed.

"We've been all through this," Kate said. "I admit that I'm a coward. But Palmer promised me, and I—"

"We're wasting time," Shanon interrupted. "Palmer hasn't backed out, anyway."

"No, I'll go through with it," Palmer called over her shoulder. She was at the mirror applying more makeup. "My lapse of confidence was only momentary. If Simmie doesn't dump his date from Brier Hall when he sees me, then he needs eyeglasses."

The girls flew down the stairs with Palmer carrying the gift-wrapped box. Other Fox Hall girls going to the dance were just gathering in the common room. "Miss Grayson's giving us punch and cookies for the road!" Brenda called out gaily.

"No thanks," Kate replied for them all.

"Just one cookie," Lisa pleaded.

Kate looked at her sharply. "No!"

The four Foxes hustled out the door with Palmer in the lead. The driver was chatting on the walk with Mr. Griffith, and the girls tried to slip by them. "Evening, ladies," Mr. Griffith said, stopping them with his deep voice. "Who's the present for?"

Palmer turned smoothly. "Something for a friend at Ardsley," she said, drowning out a soft mewing from the box.

"Get inside!" Kate whispered as they climbed into the bus.

"We almost got caught!" Lisa giggled after they found seats in the back.

"This is no laughing matter," Kate hissed.

Shanon let out a laugh. "Sorry, I'm getting the giggles."

"Me too," Amy chuckled.

"I can't help it either, hee-hee," Palmer added.

Kate slumped into her seat, mortified. The box was resting at Palmer's feet. By the time Mr. Griffith, Miss Grayson, and the rest of the girls had boarded, the Foxes were giggling uncontrollably.

"Shut up!" Kate whispered. Lisa, Shanon, Amy, and Palmer tried to oblige, but the more they muffled their laughter, the bigger the explosion.

When the bus finally stopped in front of Ardsley, they struggled to put on straight faces. "What was the big joke?" Miss Grayson asked as they got off.

"Uh, nothing," Lisa said. Palmer stood to one side holding the gift box. She could feel Tickle squirming around inside. If only the kitten wouldn't take this particular moment to meow again.

Miss Grayson eyed the box curiously.

"You know how these four can get," Kate hastily

116

explained, standing in front of Palmer to block Miss Grayson's view. "They'll laugh at anything!"

"Yes, we will!" Lisa and Shanon added in a chorus.

"And by the way, Miss Grayson," Amy added suddenly, "thanks again for letting my friend Evon stay over last weekend!"

"I'm glad it worked out," Miss Grayson replied, turning her attention to Amy. "Did the two of you have a good time?"

"Terrific," Amy said, smiling. "Evon had some interesting observations to make about Alma."

"Like what?" Miss Grayson asked.

"Well, she thought our suite's pen pals idea was great. And . . ."

While Amy struggled to hold Miss Grayson's attention, Kate nudged Palmer toward the door. Lisa and Shanon scurried behind.

"Thanks for distracting her," Kate said when Amy rejoined the other girls in front of the gym.

"No problem," Amy said. "And by the way, it looks like her date *is* Mr. Griffith."

"That's right!" Shanon agreed, glancing back over her shoulder. "If they had a fight, they must have made up. There's no sign of Mr. Seganish anywhere."

"Can we just go inside?" Palmer said impatiently. "I want to get rid of this box."

The outside of the Ardsley gymnasium looked like a fortress. Kate and the Foxes all took deep breaths before entering.

Inside, the gym wasn't nearly as intimidating. Colorful balloons and streamers hung down from the high ceilings, while taped rock music blared out from enormous speakers in each corner. Boys in dinner jackets were everywhere.

"We made it!" Kate said breathlessly. "Put the box over by the coats," she directed Palmer. "Reggie will pick it up when the time comes."

"Shouldn't we check to make sure Tickle's okay?" Shanon asked.

"We can't risk it. It's too crowded by the door now," Kate said. "There are air holes in the box—she'll be fine."

Just then, Reggie McGreevy appeared. Lisa gasped when she saw that her brother had grown a little moustache. It made him look much older.

"Hi, Reg," Kate said shyly.

"Hi, there," Reggie said, shuffling awkwardly.

"I like your moustache," Lisa said, stepping between them. "How did you grow it?"

"Hi, Sis," Reggie mumbled, not answering her question.

Kate motioned to the box on the floor beneath the coat rack.

"I've got you," Reggie said quietly.

"I'll sneak her out of here at the break," said Kate.

Palmer, Shanon, and Amy drifted away. "I'm glad my part is over," Palmer said. "I can't believe that *Kate Majors* asked *me* to break a rule!"

"Her love for animals is greater than her love for rules," Shanon observed philosophically.

Lisa came up to them. "Any sign of The Unknown yet?"

Amy's eyes swept the dance floor. "Not yet."

"What should we do?" Shanon asked. "Should we go out there and look for them? Or should we let them look for us?"

"I think I'm going to wait out in the bus," Palmer said, getting an attack of cold feet.

Amy stopped her. "No way! Your job is to show Simmie Randolph that he isn't the only boy in the world."

"Look around you," Lisa encouraged. "There are loads of Ardies here that look ten times better than Simmie. All you have to do is get one of them to dance with you."

Palmer began to panic. The original idea was to pretend that Reggie was her date. But Reggie and Kate seemed to have forgotten that.

Shanon took a deep breath. "I see Mars," she whispered. "He's coming over."

"Here comes Rob, too," Lisa exclaimed.

"Uh-oh," Amy said. "John's with them!"

The three Unknowns were dressed almost identically in dinner jackets with black string ties. For effect, Rob was wearing blue hightops and Mars sported a button that said BE HAPPY! John had a yellow flower in his hand.

Amy was the first to speak. "Hi. How's the D.J.?"

"Into heavy metal," John said, holding out the flower. "This is for you."

Amy grinned and accepted the daffodil. "Thanks."

"What do you say we all dance?" Rob said enthusiastically. He smiled at Lisa and took her hand.

"I'm up for it," Mars said, looking at Shanon. "It's great

119

to see you again," he whispered, coming close to her. As the three girls glanced at each other and giggled, Palmer stepped out of the circle and walked away.

"Where are you going?" Amy called.

"For something to drink," Palmer replied, walking away quickly. She was embarrassed enough being here without a real date. At least she could pretend to be doing something. Pasting a smile on her face, she sought out the refreshments. So far, she hadn't seen Simmie. But Reggie was coming her way.

"Are those little sandwiches any good?" he asked awkwardly.

"I haven't had one," Palmer replied.

He stared at her. "Am I supposed to be doing something special? To pretend you're my date?"

"How do I know?" Palmer snapped in frustration. "How do I know what I'm even doing here?"

Reggie touched his moustache nervously. "Kate's checking on the cat. I'm supposed to get a sandwich with tuna fish."

Suddenly, across the floor, Palmer spied Simmie. He was dancing with a pretty, dark-haired girl. Palmer laughed loudly in Reggie's direction and tried to look happy. She wanted Simmie to know she could have a good time without him.

"Is something funny?" Reggie asked.

"No, ha, ha," Palmer replied. Out of the corner of her eye, she saw Simmie watching her. He and his date had stopped dancing.

All at once, Kate came tearing across the floor. "Reggie, have you seen her?" she asked in alarm.

"Who?"

"Tickle!" Kate exclaimed. "She's gone! She's out on the dance floor!"

"There she is," Palmer said, pointing. The kitten was edging along the room near Simmie.

"Get her," Kate commanded Palmer.

"You go," Palmer said to Reggie.

"I can't see her very well," Reggie explained, squinting through his glasses.

The D.J. changed music and the sound of heavy metal blared through the speakers. With a terrified yelp, Tickle flew into the crowd.

"She's going to get trampled," Kate said, rushing out hysterically.

"I'll catch her," Palmer said, running onto the floor.

The kitten was scurrying amidst the dancers' feet, and Palmer scooped her up before she got stepped on. "It's okay, kitty," she said gently.

Simmie appeared at her side with the dark-haired girl right behind him. He smiled at Palmer. "What's wrong, doesn't he like the music?"

"It's a she," Palmer replied, looking him dead in the eye.

Simmie cleared his throat. "This is Gail," he said. "She goes to Brier Hall."

Palmer nodded, and the girl smiled nicely.

"This is my pen pal, Palmer Durand," Simmie said, completing the introduction.

"Would you like some punch?" the Brier Hall girl asked Simmie cheerfully.

Simmie gave her a grin. "I'd love some, babe. You go get it. I'll join you in a second."

The girl returned Simmie's smile. Palmer noticed again how pretty she was. "Would you like some, too?" she asked Palmer.

"No thank you," Palmer said, trying to sound sweet.

Once Simmie and Palmer were alone, they stared at each other. "I didn't expect to see you," Simmie said with a nervous chuckle. "Who's your date?"

Palmer almost said Reggie but stopped herself. "She is," she replied, stroking Tickle's soft fur.

"Very funny," Simmie chortled. "But I'm sure you had to come with an Ardie and not a cat."

Palmer felt her heart beating faster. She wanted to say so many things, but she couldn't get any of them out. She was ready to tell him that he'd hurt her feelings and that he'd been mean to psyche her out during the tennis match. But the words wouldn't come.

Simmie grabbed her arm. "Let's dance."

"What about your date?" Palmer said sarcastically. The girl from Brier Hall was heading their way with two punch cups.

"Forget about her," Simmie said smoothly. "Inviting her was a mistake. You're the one I should have asked. I know that now."

Palmer flushed. It was exactly what she'd wanted to hear. "I don't think it was very nice of you to psyche me out like you did," she said, feeling as if her throat was closing up. "I've had very hurt feelings."

Simmie laughed. "What can I say? I'm a creep," he joked.

Reggie and Kate came over to get Tickle from Palmer. "I'll take her over to the kitchen now," Reggie said.

"The cook here at Ardsley is going to adopt her," Kate explained.

The music slowed down then. Palmer and Simmie moved closer and started to dance.

"Wow!" Amy murmured from the other side of the floor. She, Shanon, and Lisa had just come out of the ladies' room. "Looks like Palmer has got Simmie Randolph back!"

"She's beaten the competition from Brier Hall," Lisa said.

"How could he resist?" Shanon said breathlessly. "Palmer looks so gorgeous in that dress."

The girls gazed around the room and spotted Mars, John, and Rob coming toward them with plates of sandwiches. Kate and Reggie were leaving together with Tickle. Even Miss Grayson was starting a dance with Mr. Griffith.

"This is perfect!" Lisa said dreamily. "We've *all* got dates!"

CHAPTER FOURTEEN

Dear Palmer babe,
  Was it ever fortunite that you showed up at the dance. You rescued me from the most boring girl ever. You're the raining princess of my heart.

                                          Love,
                                          Simmie

Dear Shanon,
  Good news. My dad has another job. And this one is better. So I guess we're not going to be bankrupt, and I can stay at Ardsley. That's what was in the back of my mind, that I might have to quit. But we're in the black again. And the buttons are taking off. In fact, I'm going to have to get somebody to go in with me to increase production. Also, I might branch out into T-shirts. I've got some on order for the other guys in the suite with "The Unknown" written on them.
  I sent a note to your father asking him about the garage position. The summer is far off, but it's not too early to

plan. Are you going to be living at home? That might influence my decision. In other words, I'd like to see more of you. For a while I had the notion that you were just thinking of me as a friend. But after the dance I think maybe you're thinking of me as something more. Is that true? Your pink dress was nice and so is your long hair. Don't ever cut it. So now I'm a girls' fashion expert, right?

Shanon, thanks for getting me out of the dumps. Nobody has ever done that for me. Once I'm in one of my moods, be it mad, sad, up or down, nobody can get me out of it. But you did. It is hard for me to write this. I think I sound like an idiot. But I'm trying to be real, just like you are. You're great. And if you ever need somebody to write to about something on your mind, I'd be glad to be the person.

Love,
Mars

P.S. Enclosed are some buttons for you and the other Foxes.

Dear Mars,

That was the nicest letter anyone ever sent me. I'm glad my dad is interested in your possibly working for him. Thus far, my plan is to be at home this summer. I have applied to get in a special training program for stringers with this magazine in New York, however. I won't hear about that for a while. I'll be up against people with a lot more experience, so I might not get it. If I don't, I'll be working in the convenience store connected to my dad's business. Thank you for the buttons and thank you for *inviting me to the dance. I had a wonderful time. As for whether I consider you just a friend or something more, the answer is yes. Yes, I consider you something more.*

Yours truly,
Shanon

Dear Lisa,

Good news! The summer job in Alaska fell through, so I'll be working in Pennsylvania on the dairy farm after all. Also, I was wondering if you would be my girlfriend.

Love,
Rob

P.S. One thing for sure—you are better than a musk ox!

Dear Rob,

Too bad about your not getting to go to Alaska. It is great that you are going to be in Pennsylvania, but I want you to know that if another opportunity comes along and you have to work in another state, I will not stand in your way. It is all right if you don't work in Pennsylvania. That isn't to say that I'm not happy that you are going to be working there. And as to that question you asked. I think I want to be your girlfriend. At least while I am at Alma.

Sincerely,
Lisa

Dear Amy,

I am sitting at my desk thinking of a new poem. It would be about an independent thirteen-year-old woman with jet black hair. You have become my muse. Let's make a pact not to fight each other anymore. I loved the music at the dance. How about you?

Love,
John

Dear John,

To be called someone's muse is the highest compliment. If men are muses also, you are my muse, too. When you mentioned independence in your letter, it stirred my head with a song. I'll run it by you once I've got something. I'm so used to people telling me what not to do. Before I came to Alma that was the case with my dad especially. So maybe that's why I was so ready to call you a chauvinist.

I loved coming to the dance, but I hated the music. My taste is veering away from the real heavy stuff. And it would be nice to have a live band, not just taped music. But it's just my opinion. I don't want to fight about it. In fact, I hope we can continue to collaborate musically. I do think it is important that we have the freedom to express our opinions, however. My opinion of you is that you are a one-of-a-kind person who I am glad to know and look forward to knowing even better.

Yours truly,
Amy

"Did you notice how all four of them signed their letters 'love'?" Shanon said, starry-eyed.

"Lisa got the best response," Amy declared. "Rob just

127

came right out and said he wanted her to be his girlfriend!"

"Why did you say it was all right if he didn't work in Pennsylvania?" Shanon asked. "I thought that was what you wanted."

"It was," Lisa said, flustered. "But now that he's actually asked me to be his girlfriend, I don't know."

"I thought you wanted to be his girlfriend," Amy insisted.

"I did!" Lisa agreed. "But now that I am, I wonder what it means. I've never been anybody's girlfriend before. It's heavy. First I had a pen pal, now I have a boyfriend, and this summer he might be living in the same state with me."

Amy chuckled. "You're so contradictory. First you say you'd go anywhere in the world to be with Rob and now you're scared of getting in too deep."

"I understand how Lisa could be nervous," Shanon piped up. "It's deep having a boyfriend."

"But we're the Foxes of the Third Dimension," Amy argued. "The third dimension is depth! Remember?"

"Let's not talk about me and Rob anymore," Lisa cut in. "What I'd like to know is why Amy's always picking fights with John."

"I distinctly said in my letter to John that I didn't want to fight," Amy argued. "But I have to be free to state my opinions."

Lisa shook her head. "You're never going to get any more letters that way."

"I think I'm going to order some T-shirts from Mars that say 'The Foxes of the Third Dimension,'" Shanon said dreamily. "He's only thirteen, and he's already a business-man."

"Simmie Randolph's fourteen and he's already a jerk!" Lisa interjected.

"To each her own," Amy said with a shrug. "Palmer's crazy about him."

"And Simmie's crazy about her," Shanon added. "That letter he sent after the dance proves it. Even if it *was* full of misspellings. I wonder if—"

Shanon broke off guiltily as Palmer walked into the suite carrying her tennis racket. "I saw Kate on my way in," she reported. "She got a letter from Reggie and he said that Tickle is happily settling in at the Ardsley kitchen. She even caught a mouse."

"Incredible," Lisa said. "Tickle's the first female to live at the place."

Shanon laughed. "Maybe she'll start going to classes."

Palmer sat down on the loveseat.

"Don't sit down," Amy said. "We've been waiting for you to get choc-shots."

"We've been discussing our pen pals, too," Shanon said.

"I thought that boys weren't going to be the main topic of conversation anymore," Palmer said wryly.

"It's all right to discuss boys as long as it doesn't take over our lives," Lisa declared. "By the way, did you send your answer to Simmie?"

"Nope," Palmer said.

"What are you waiting for?" Amy asked. "We sent our answers to the other Unknowns a couple of days ago."

Palmer got up and walked to the desk. "Okay, I'll send my answer to Simmie right now." She picked up a piece of notepaper and began folding it.

"What are you doing?" Shanon asked. "You haven't even written anything."

"You'll see," Palmer said. Completing her task, she held up a perfect paper airplane. Then, with a sharp snap of her arm, she sent it arcing out the open window.

Lisa giggled. "What's the big idea?"

"That's my answer to Simmie's letter," Palmer said with a shrug. "Air mail."

"But it was a blank piece of paper," Amy said.

"I've decided not to be pen pals with Simmie Randolph anymore," Palmer told them. "I'm not even going to write and say that I don't want to write."

Lisa whistled. "That's a serious decision. When did you make it?"

"It took me a while," Palmer said, turning away. "But after all is said and done, Simmie's a creep. Why would I want a creep for a pen pal? Why would I even want to know one?"

"Fantastic," Amy cheered. "I agree with you. Especially after the way he made you lose the round robin."

"He didn't make me lose," Palmer admitted. "He did try to psyche me out, but I'm the one who lost the point. I talked to Coach Barker about it this morning. I'm off the team."

"Oh, no!" Shanon wailed. "That isn't fair. It wasn't your fault."

"It *was* my fault," Palmer said. "The least I could do

130

was be honest about it and clear my conscience. Anyway, there's another reason I don't want to know Randolph."

"What's that?" Lisa asked curiously.

"The way he treated that girl from Brier Hall!" Palmer exclaimed. "First I was happy that he wanted to dance with me instead of her. But then I realized that it could have been the other way around. *I* could have been his date. Then I would have been the one to get dumped. It was too humiliating for her! I don't ever want that to happen to me."

"So that's it?" Lisa said.

Palmer sighed. "Yes, that's it. I'm off the tennis team and out of a pen pal."

"You'll find something else to do," Shanon said sympathetically. "There's that tutoring project coming up."

"Tutoring project?"

"Don't you remember?" Shanon prodded. "The community-service project? You volunteered. It'll be fun."

"I guess. . . ." Palmer replied.

"And you have to have another pen pal," Lisa insisted. "You're still one of the Foxes."

"I am?" Palmer's eyebrows rose questioningly.

"Of course. All for one and one for all!" Amy said. "There are four Foxes of the Third Dimension and that's the way it always will be."

"Lisa's right, we'll just have to find you another pen pal," Shanon said.

"And if it helps," Lisa added, "I have a lot of respect for your decision not to write to Simmie."

"And for telling Coach Barker how you sacrificed the

131

match," Amy added. "That took a lot of nerve."

Palmer smiled. Amy, Lisa, and Shanon were all looking at her as if they really liked her. As if she were still important in spite of everything that had happened. "Thanks, you guys," she said happily. "You make me feel better."

"Let's go get a choc-shot!" Lisa yelled.

"Wait a minute!" Palmer said in a commanding voice. "I have to comb my hair first."

"Don't forget to check your makeup," Amy teased.

"And while you're at it," Shanon said, giggling, "put on a fresh outfit."

Palmer laughed loudly. "You're all making fun of me!"

"That's because we like you," Amy said.

"I *am* going to change out of these clothes, though," Palmer added, heading for the bedroom. "I think the idea of my getting a new pen pal is really exciting! I just hope it doesn't end up being someone like Simmie."

"We'll do our best," Lisa assured her. "We'll put an ad in the Ardsley paper again and this time we'll get your ideal pen pal!"

"What is your ideal pen pal?" Amy asked.

Palmer turned and stood in the doorway. "Handsome, rich, and not a creep," she stated firmly.

"We'll ask them to send in their pictures so we can check out their looks," Amy said. "And most of the boys at Ardsley come from families with a lot of money."

"But how are we going to make sure the boy isn't a creep?" Shanon asked.

"No problem!" Lisa said, waving her hand. "We'll put it all in the advertisement."

Palmer quickly changed her clothes and the Foxes headed off to the snack bar. On the way, Shanon passed out the buttons from Mars: READ MY MIND! for Amy; BE HAPPY! for Lisa; BE REAL! for Palmer; and, for herself, I'D RATHER BE EATING CHOCOLATE!

"What an incredible day!" Amy exclaimed, breathing in the spring air. "Only one thing could make it more perfect."

"What's that?" Shanon asked.

"If my friend Evon were here, too," Amy replied. "Her visit was so short. Seems like we just got to know each other again and she had to leave."

"Too bad she lives so far away," Shanon said.

"I know," sighed Amy. "I wish I could see her more often. I guess we'll just have to keep writing letters."

"Speaking of letters . . ." Palmer chimed in, sidling up next to Lisa. "Do you really think I can get another pen pal?"

Lisa's dark eyes twinkled. "I've already thought of what to put in the paper." She whispered something in Palmer's ear and began giggling.

"Great!" Palmer shrieked.

"Tell me!" Amy demanded. Palmer whispered in Amy's ear and Amy whispered to Shanon. By the time they reached the snack bar, the four Foxes were all laughing in agreement over the advertisement. There was another thing they agreed on that nobody talked about. After months of ups and downs at Alma Stephens, they were no longer just four girls living in the same suite, or even just the Foxes of the Third Dimension. They were four good friends.

WANTED: BOY PEN PAL FOR ATTRACTIVE GIRL AT ALMA STEPHENS
MUST BE MIND READER: N. C. N. A.*
SEND PICTURE AND QUALIFICATIONS TO FOXES OF THE THIRD DIMENSION
IN CARE OF THE ALMA LEDGER, ALMA STEPHENS SCHOOL FOR GIRLS.

* no creeps need apply

Something to write home about . . .
                              four new Pen Pals stories!

In Book Five, the pen pal-less Palmer seeks a replacement for Simmie Randolph III. It seems that lots of Ardsley boys would like to get to know the beautiful blonde from Alma Stephens. All Palmer has to do is pick one . . .
    Here is a scene from Pen Pals #5: SAM THE SHAM:

The four Foxes gathered in a circle on the sitting-room floor of Suite 3–D. Palmer arranged the letters in front of her according to color so that they looked like a rainbow.

"Well," Lisa prodded, "start reading."

"I will, I will," Palmer said. "Don't rush me. This is a very important moment in my life. Who knows what sort of boy I may meet!"

Despite Palmer's haughty attitude, Lisa was glad to see the sparkle back in her friend's eyes. Though all the Foxes had applauded Palmer when she stopped speaking—and writing—to Simmie, they soon learned that a Palmer without a boy in her life was not the most pleasant person to live with. Somewhat self-absorbed and snobbish in the best of times, she could be absolutely impossible when the going got tough.

But now, fortunately, things seemed to be looking up.

"Just pick one!" Amy pleaded. "I can't stand the suspense."

"All right." As Palmer reached for a mysterious black envelope, all the girls held their breath. But she didn't open it. Instead she tossed it into the wastebasket she'd dragged out of her bedroom.

"What did you do that for?" Lisa demanded. "You didn't even read it."

"I can tell he wouldn't be my type," Palmer said. "He's probably an undertaker's son or something just as gross."

"I thought it looked interesting," Amy murmured, her eyes drifting wistfully toward the wastebasket.

"You would," Palmer groaned, giving Amy's all-black outfit a disdainful look before picking up a pale blue envelope. Carefully, she ran one pink-polished thumbnail under the flap. She read the letter silently, then threw it into the trash too.

Palmer quickly ripped open nine more letters, none of which met with her approval. And then, at last, she found one worth sharing. "Listen to this," she said.

Dear Palmer,
My name is Sam O'Leary. Here's my picture. Hope you think it's okay because I'd really like to be your special friend. My interests include sports (I play lacrosse, and swim, and ski). I like dancing a lot, too, but I don't get to do it much because I'm too busy making music. I've played

the guitar and drums since I was six. Now I have my own rock band. A lot of girls think it's cool to hang around with musicians for the prestige. I want to find a girl who likes me for myself. Please write.

Sam

Handsome, talented, and super-cool, Sam looks and sounds just about perfect. Lisa, Shanon, and Amy couldn't be happier for Palmer—until she becomes so involved with her new pen pal that she forgets all about her old friends.

PEN PALS #6:   AMY'S SONG

The Alma Stephens School is buzzing with excitement— the girls are going to London! Amy is most excited of all. She and her pen pal John have written a song together, and one of the Ardsley boys has arranged for her to sing it in a London club. It's the chance of a lifetime! But once in London, the girls are constantly supervised, and Amy can't see how she'll ever get away to the club. She and her suitemates plot and scheme to get out from under the watchful eye of their chaperone, but it's harder than they thought it would be. It looks as if Amy will never get her big break!

PEN PALS #7:   HANDLE WITH CARE

Shanon is tired of standing in Lisa's shadow. She wants to be thought of as her own person. So she decides to run for student council representative—against Lisa! Lisa not only feels abandoned by her best friend, but by her pen pal, too. While the election seems to be bringing Shanon and Mars closer together, it's definitely driving Lisa and Rob apart.

Lisa's sure she'll win the election. After all, she's always been a leader—shy Shanon's the follower. Or is she? Will the election spoil the girls' friendship? And will it mean the end of Rob and Lisa?

PEN PALS #8:   SEALED WITH A KISS

When the Ardsley and Alma drama departments join forces to produce a rock musical, Lisa and Amy audition just for fun. Lisa lands a place in the chorus, but Amy gets a leading role. Lisa can't help feeling a little jealous, especially when her pen pal Rob also gets a leading role—opposite Amy. To make matters worse, the director wants Rob and Amy to kiss! Amy is so caught up in the play that she doesn't notice Lisa's jealousy—at first. And when she finally does notice, the damage has already been done!

P.S. Have you missed any Pen Pals? Catch up now!

PEN PALS #1:   BOYS WANTED

Suitemates Lisa, Shanon, Amy, and Palmer love the Alma Stephens School for Girls. There's only one problem—no boys! So the girls put an ad in the newspaper of the nearby Ardsley Academy for Boys asking for male pen pals. Soon their mailboxes are flooded with letters and photos from Ardsley boys, but the girls choose four boys from a suite just like their own. Through their letters, the girls learn a lot about their new pen pals—and about themselves.

PEN PALS #2:   TOO CUTE FOR WORDS

Palmer, the rich girl from Florida, has never been one for playing by the rules. So when she wants Amy's pen pal,

Simmie, instead of her own, she simply takes him. She writes to Simmie secretly, and soon he stops writing to Amy. When Shanon, Lisa, and Amy find out why, the suite is in an uproar. How could Palmer be so deceitful? Before long, Palmer is thinking of leaving the suite—and the other girls aren't about to stop her. Where will it all end?

PEN PALS #3:   P.S. FORGET IT!

Palmer is out to prove that her pen pal is the best—and her suitemate Lisa's is a jerk. When Lisa receives strange letters and a mysterious prank gift, it looks as if Palmer may be right. But does she have to be so smug about it? Soon it's all-out war in Suite 3-D!

From the sidelines, Shanon and Amy think something fishy is going on. Is the pen pal scheme going too far? Will it stop before Lisa does something she may regret? Or will the girls learn to settle their differences?